CRY APACHES!

CRY APACHES!

A ' Catsfoot ' Western

by

JOHN ROBB

THE CHILDREN'S PRESS
LONDON AND GLASGOW

This edition 1968

For Anthony

PRINTED AND MADE IN GREAT BRITAIN

CONTENTS

ILLUSTRATIONS

CHAPTER ONE

THE LAST STAND

IT HAD always been a hopeless battle. Now the end was near. Hideously near . . .

Crouched amid the sagebrush on the southern bank of the Gila River, the troopers formed a single defence line against the Mescalero Apaches. At the start of the day, when they had first been trapped, that line had stretched more than a hundred paces from flank to flank. But, in the ghastly hours of struggle, it had shortened. The line had shrunk as survivors closed in to make good the gaps left by casualties.

A mere sixteen troopers remained, plus a bugle boy. Their faces smoke-smeared and weary, they awaited the next attack. And they knew it would be the last one. The remnants of Lieutenant Anderson's column of the Fourth Cavalry were no longer strong enough to throw back the might of the huge Apache war party.

Lieutenant Anderson's tunic was wet with blood from a shoulder wound. He rose to a knee and put a pair of glasses to his eyes. After a few moments he said to his column sergeant: "There're still a heck of a lot of Indians out there. It looks like this is where we say good-bye."

"I guess so, lieutenant, but I figure we've given a good account of ourselves."

"We had just one thing in our favour—the river at our backs. If it hadn't been for the river, we wouldn't have lasted as long as this." He paused, then asked: "How's the ammunition?"

"There's not much left, sir, but there's plenty."

Anderson gave the N.C.O. a puzzled stare. "What the heck are you talking about?"

"I mean that we're runnin' short, but that don't need to worry us any. The Apaches'll have us before we can loose off what we've got."

Anderson put his field glasses back in their leather case. Then he took his ·44 Remington revolver from its Gaylord holster. He spun the cylinder, checking the chambers.

"My gun's full, sergeant . . . but I'm going to try to keep one shot for myself and I guess the rest of you'd better try to do the same. It'll be better than being caught alive by the Apaches."

"Mebbe so, lieutenant, but . . . I'm wonderin'. . ."

"Go on! What's on your mind?"

"It's Steve Reynold, sir, the bugle kid. He's no more'n a boy. What about him?"

They looked backwards, to a spot on the edge of the river bank. There Steve Reynold, a field medical box at his side, was adjusting a bandage on a trooper's hand. His silver bugle hung from a white cord at his waist.

"We can't allow him to be captured alive, either,"

Anderson said. "He's very young, but that won't make any difference to the Apaches."

"That's just what I was thinkin', sir."

Anderson called to Steve: "Hey, kid! I want to talk with you."

Steve made a last check of the bandage. Then, snapping shut the medical box, he joined the lieutenant and the sergeant. Anderson looked thoughtfully at the boy, whose dark and curly hair showed from under his blue peaked army cap. He noted that the boy's normally cheerful face had become as strained and weary as the others'.

"How old are you, kid?"

"Just fifteen, sir."

"That's not so very old, but you've done mighty well looking after the wounded. Mebbe you'd have made a good cavalry man. I guess you didn't expect to finish up this way when you enlisted as a bugle blow."

Steve said: "I always knew there was a chance of it happening, sir. You see, I know quite a bit about the Apaches."

"You do, uh! How come?"

"They killed my mom and pop, sir."

There was a short, uneasy silence while Anderson and the sergeant stared at the ground. Then Anderson said: "You know we haven't a hope? We're outnumbered by more than twenty to one and there's no help going to come from anywhere."

Steve wiped grimy sweat from his forehead with the back of his hand. Then he said in a whisper: "I guess we've all known that all day, sir . . . that's why I'd like to ask a favour."

"Right now, I ain't exactly equipped to grant favours, kid. But what is it?"

"Will you let me have a rifle, sir?"

Anderson fought down a spasm of pain from his shoulder wound before saying: "Regulations don't allow bugle boys to carry guns. When we're in action, your job's to look after the medical box."

"I know . . . but I guess I'm goin' to die like all the rest of us."

"Yeah, there's no sense pretending anything else. We're all finished."

Steve's face was twitching as he said quickly: "Then I want to die like a *man*, sir! I figure I've a right to go down with a gun in my hand, like the rest of you!"

Their eyes met. Then Anderson stretched towards a small pile of equipment which had been removed from the casualties. He picked up a revolver, passed it to Steve.

"That's yours. From now on you're a real soldier. There are six shells in there, but you'd best keep one of them to use on yourself, like we all plan to do. Mebbe you know what the Apaches do to cavalry men if they take us alive."

Steve weighed the weapon in his hand, then pushed it under his belt. He began: "They won't take . . ."

But he never completed the sentence. He was interrupted by a sudden shout from the sergeant.

"Look! They're comin' for us, right now, sir!"

And they were. A thousand yards away, a thin barrier of dust billowed and swirled, thrown up by hundreds of advancing hooves. For the moment, that dust concealed the Apaches, so that it seemed as if no more than a fantastic storm cloud was approaching.

A sigh went up from the short line of troopers. Mainly, it was a sigh of relief. The waiting agony was almost over. One more blood-laden clash was to come—just a few seconds of chaos and terror. Then all would be finished.

The troopers raised their Spencer carbines and some of them stroked the barrels. The feel of those weapons was comforting. Holding one of them, a man could sell his life at a high price, for they were the most powerful and accurate repeaters issued to the United States Army.

There was a series of mechanical clicks as each trooper jerked his combined cranking-lever and trigger-guard down, then up, forcing a rim-fire cartridge into the breech.

His voice clear and steady, Anderson shouted: "Sight two hundred!"

The troopers adjusted the back sights of their carbines to a range of two hundred yards. In the ordinary way, that would be an excessively long range against fast-moving targets. But the Apaches were attacking in closely-packed lines, making it almost impossible to miss them.

Now they could be seen clearly. They were

crouched forward over their ponies and their faces were made hideous by the crimson and yellow war dyes on them. Their long hair streamed in the wind and they clutched battle lances, tomahawks, and a variety of captured muskets and rifles. The sound of hooves was like the approach of distant thunder.

Steve, knowing that his revolver would be useless until the last moment, lay flat on the sage. The rest of the cavalrymen were doing the same—except Anderson. The officer remained kneeling, eyes never leaving the Apaches as he calculated distance before giving the last order.

Four hundred yards . . .

The noise was beginning to press on the eardrums. It seemed that nothing known to man could halt the impetus of that attack. Steve could not help wondering whether there was any point in bothering to open fire. Surely it would be better for all if the Apaches were allowed to come without hindrance, so that it would all be over as soon as possible? Steve forced the thought from his mind, blaming himself for cowardice.

Anderson raised his left hand. In answer to the signalled order, the troopers thumbed back the hammers of their Spencers. They were all toughened Indian fighters, those troopers. There was not a raw recruit among them. They were afraid, as all men are afraid when facing an awful end. But their fear had been conquered by courage and discipline. Their faces were calm, their hands steady.

Suddenly, above the gathering tumult, Anderson shouted: "Prepare for seven round rapid . . . !"

Fingers took first pressure on triggers. Ears strained to catch the one word which would complete the order. It came at last, faintly and almost lost amid the gathering crash of hooves.

"*Fire. . . !*"

Sixteen scarlet flashes spat out of the gas vents of sixteen Spencer carbines. Steve heard a massed explosion, as though the skies were being ripped apart. And he saw ghastly gaps torn in the lines of Apaches. Ponies reared and fell, bringing down others in the files directly behind, causing pockets of utter chaos. But the speed of the charge did not slacken.

With trained precision, the troopers again worked the cranking levers, ejecting empty shells and bringing forward new rounds from the butt magazines. Their second volley was more lethal than the first, for the range was now much closer. A thin haze of blue smoke was rising from the little line of troopers. The acrid smell of burnt powder tainted the hot air.

For a few uncertain seconds it seemed as if a miracle might happen—as if the assault would be thrown back. For in isolated places, where casualties had been heaviest, the Apaches wavered. Some even tried to turn their ponies for a retreat, but they were prevented from doing so by the onrush of those behind. The troopers, seeing this, delivered a third and fourth volley so quickly that the roar of the explosions merged into each other.

But the Apaches recovered. It was as if the temporary set-back had further enraged them. In an almost solid body, they lashed their ponies to greater speed. And a new sound joined that of thundering hooves and reverberating explosions. It was a wild, satanic screaming from hundreds of Apache throats.

Steve thought: "They're here . . . this is it!"

He jumped to his feet. All the troopers were now standing, too. In a vague, nightmarish way, he was aware of a wall of animals sweeping towards him, threatening to crush him. He saw a soldier throw himself against that wall, then vanish into the midst of it. He glimpsed the sergeant, holding his carbine by the barrel and swinging it like a club, suddenly fall under one of the Apaches' mounts, a lance deep in his back. As though from far off, Steve heard a thin crack from Anderson's revolver. That reminded him that he, too, had a gun. He must use it—first on the Apaches, then on himself. . . .

He tried to aim at the wall of Indians. But he did not have the time to do so. An Apache, scalping knife glittering in one hand, was directly upon him. Steve tried to jump aside. The pony caught him a glancing blow on the chest which lifted him high into the air. At the same moment, Steve saw the curved knife slash past his throat.

He felt as if he were a stone hurled from a catapult as he somersaulted through space. He landed on his stomach with a force which seemed to push his spine out of his body. Now he was rolling like a wagon wheel and he could not understand what was happening to him, for his brain was numbed. It sprang to life again when an icy shock gripped his entire body and he spluttered and choked for breath. It was then that he knew that he must have rolled down the slight incline and into the river.

The River Gila was deep here. And it had a fast current, which was already sweeping him into midstream. Immediately, Steve realised that his one slender chance of survival lay in keeping close to the bank, where he might be invisible to the Apaches. He spotted a small piece of land, thickly covered with yellow-flowering Prickly Pear cactus, which overhung the water. If he could get under that . . .

But his uniform and equipment were a dead weight, threatening to pull him under. The heavy riding boots were the greatest threat, for they had filled with water and were holding it. Being tightly laced, there was no chance of kicking them off.

He turned on to his back and kicked out at an angle, letting the current do most of the work. His legs ached, and he had to strain to keep his mouth out of the water. He had almost decided to give up, to take the easy way out by drowning, when he saw prickly shrubs above him. Steve grasped one of them and pulled until he was pressed against soft earth.

Slowly, he lowered his feet. They met the river bottom. Here he could stand, water level with the top of his shoulders, and almost totally concealed by the cactus on the overhanging bank.

For the first time in minutes, he was able to think of the others. He knew that he had not been swept more than fifty yards from the point of entering the river. With his fingers, he squeezed water out of his ears and listened. Voices came to him—Apache voices. They were talking among themselves. All sounds of battle had vanished. All the Spencer carbines were silent.

Steve knew that there was one risk he must take— he must take a look. Cactus tore at his hands as he pulled himself partly out of the water and rested his chest on the bank. The scene before him made him close his eyes immediately. Most of the Apaches were already riding away, their work of massacre done. But a group of about two dozen were collecting the carbines which had belonged to the troopers. Others were assembling the cavalry horses from a spot where they had been tethered farther up river. And on the ground, motionless, lay huddled figures in blue.

As he slipped back into the water, Steve knew it was very unlikely that any had survived except himself. Amid the horror of it, there was the one consolation that apparently the Apaches had failed to take any of them alive.

It was dark and the moon had risen when at last he heard the remaining Apaches ride off. Trembling from exhaustion and the chill of the river, Steve again climbed on to the bank. This time, he pulled himself completely clear of the water. On his feet, he hesitated. He knew that he must return to the

place where the troopers had made their last stand.
Until he saw for himself, he could never be entirely
certain that some were not still alive and in need of
help. When that duty was done, he must try to
reach the cavalry base at Fort Coulter.

Water dripping from him, his teeth chattering,
Steve forced himself to walk towards the scene of
massacre. All the time, he fought a desire to turn
away.

He had covered about half the distance when he
heard a flap of wings. He shuddered. Already the
buzzards were there. And, from far off, there was
the mournful howling of a coyote. He felt alone and
very afraid in a dark and hostile world.

But was he alone?

The question came to Steve out of nowhere. It
brought him to an abrupt halt. His heart was
thudding and his breath coming in short, shallow
gasps.

Suddenly, without knowing why, he had the
feeling that men—living men—were near. He
listened again. The buzzards had gone, but the
coyote was still howling. To his left, there was a
steady drone from the fast-flowing river. All around
him there was the faint whisper of the breeze in the
sage.

Then he heard it; heard the unmistakable clink of
bridle chains and the gentle thud of horses being
ridden slowly and cautiously. At first, he thought
that the Apaches were returning and he braced himself to run. Then he realised that this was unlikely,

since Indian ponies did not carry steel bridles. In any case, if Redskins were returning, they would not do so with such obvious care. There could be but one explanation—a party of whites had arrived. This piece of territory was well away from the marked trails, but occasionally copper miners followed the banks of the Gila when on their way to the trading post near Fort Coulter.

Steve knew a rush of relief. Pulling in a deep breath, he gave a meaningless shout. Then he rushed forward.

Suddenly, in the moonlight, he saw it. He saw the remains of those who had been his comrades sprawled on the sage. And, in the middle of what had been the defence line, he saw three men standing beside their horses. Their faces were turned towards him and they glinted palely. Each of them was holding a gun and each gun was levelled at Steve.

One of them shouted: "Hold it! Stop right where you are!"

Steve came to a stumbling stop. He called back: "It's all right! I'm Steve Reynold of . . ."

"Okay. Come on nice and slow."

The voice was harsh.

Steve moved towards them at a steady walk, keeping his eyes fixed on them. As they came more clearly into view, he saw that the three were standing with their legs well parted, their guns held slightly forward from the hip. It was understandable that they should keep him covered until he had fully identified himself, but there was something strangely menacing about those men. It gave Steve his first flicker of new fear.

He stopped when only a yard away from them. Now he could see their every detail. They were strikingly alike, those men. All three were of no more than ordinary height. But they had massive shoulders and immense chests which suggested bull-like strength. Their faces were square, the features crude. Each had eyes which showed as black slits.

Steve looked at their guns. A lot could be learned from the way a man held his gun. These three held them with easy familiarity, as if they were part of them.

The man in the centre said: "You got any friends around?"

Steve shook his head. "The column's been cut to pieces. I guess I'm the only one left alive."

"Too bad . . . by the look of you, I figure you hid in the river."

"That's the way it was."

There was a short burst of laughter. Then another said:

"You were smart to run away, kid. There ain't no sense being a dead hero."

"But I didn't run! I was knocked . . ."

"Sure, sure! But you're a bit young to be a tin soldier, ain't you?"

"I'm an enlisted bugler and my name's Steve, like I told you. Right now, I'll ask you folks to help me see if any of the troopers are still living."

"You can save your time. We've already had a good look around."

"So there's no one . . . ?"

"They're dead, all of 'em." He paused, then added slowly: "And it's a good thing, too."

Steve blinked at him.

"Mebbe I didn't hear you right, mister," he said.

"You heard okay. I told you it's a good thing them tin soldiers are dead."

Steve felt the blood drain out of his face and his throat become dry. "You're crazy," he muttered. "The army's here to protect all of us."

"It ain't here to protect us. We don't like soldiers any more than the Apaches do—and that goes for kid buglers, too."

"But why? Who are you?"

The three men looked at each other, humourless smiles on their hard faces. The one who had first spoken to Steve said: "Ever heard of the Brogan brothers?"

At first, Steve stared at them in bewildered disbelief. Then memories flooded back. Stories of the three Brogan Brothers had been told at Fort Coulter and at most other places in Arizona Territory. Often they were retailed in hushed tones, with uneasy glances around, for it was rumoured that the Brogans always hunted down any man who spoke against them.

They were the worst example of the breed of outlaws who were exploiting the chaos in Arizona in these years directly following the Civil War.

During that war, all soldiers had been withdrawn from the territory. The result was that the Apache tribes had broken out of their reservations and, with no one to stop them, had massacred whole white populations. It became known as "Terror Territory." Only in the larger cities, such as Phoenix and Tucson, where settlers organised their own defence forces, were white people able to live in safety.

When peace was restored between the Northern and Southern states, President Grant immediately ordered troops back to Arizona. But the army was short of men. Forts, which had been destroyed by the Apaches during their absence, had to be rebuilt. Badly needed military supplies were often destroyed by Apaches long before reaching their destination. The pitifully small garrisons had the next-to-impossible task of restoring order over a vast and hostile territory. There were times when it seemed as if, by sheer weight of numbers, the Apaches would either completely destroy the army, or force a general retreat from Arizona.

But Indians were not the only menace to the territory. There were whites, too, who had established their own brand of terror. Taking advantage of the fact that the forces of law were strained almost to breaking point, they bushwhacked stages, robbed assay offices and banks, and had even been known to raid the smaller wagon trains.

Between these renegade whites and the Apaches there sometimes existed an uneasy partnership. Neither trusted the other, but each recognised the other as being temporarily useful. Thus it occasionally happened that outlaw whites were safe from Indian attack.

Whites like the Brogan Brothers. . . .

But the Brogans stood apart. They were supreme in their evil. They not only conducted robberies with daring efficiency. They also killed without reason. It was said that no man could draw faster than they. Several courageous law officers had tried to do so, including a posse led by the famous Marshal Werner, of Elephant Butt. All had died before the lightning guns of the Brogans.

A few lines of verse suddenly hammered through Steve's brain. He remembered hearing them at Fort Coulter. They were said to be the swaggering motto of the brothers.

> *"We're not scared of posse men,*
> *No matter what their size,*
> *If they talk rough*
> *We call their bluff,*
> *And with slugs we equalise."*

Steve remembered, too, that no one knew for certain the first names of the three. They had never been heard to refer to each other by name. It was as if, knowing that they looked very alike, they sought to cause further confusion by losing all individuality.

All this flashed through Steve's mind in a few tense seconds. Then he realised that one of them was talking again.

"I figure you must be feelin' kind of worried, now

you know who we are," he was saying. "Well, you sure have plenty to be worried about, kid."

"Why? You . . . you're not going to harm me?"

"Aren't we!"

"But why should you? All I want is to get to the fort and make a report."

"Listen, kid, you ain't goin' to make any report to any fort. It so happens that a certain hombre's due this way any time and we're lookin' forward to meetin' up with him. We're goin' to exchange compliments with him, see? Compliments with guns. But we want it to be a nice surprise for him and we ain't takin' the chance of you meetin' him first and givin' him a warnin'."

Steve tried to swallow a big lump in his throat.

"You mean . . . you mean you're waiting here to kill a man?"

"You catch on fast."

"But why? One man won't have a chance against the three of you!"

"We don't give chances. This hombre's a trail scout. He's just been paid off after bringin' a wagon train into Fort Coulter and he's heavy with dollars. Got it?"

Steve understood well enough. Trail scouts were sometimes paid off at the fort after guiding wagon trains south from the Oregon Trail. After months of dangerous work, during which the lives of scores of people were in their hands, they usually received a settlement of more than a thousand dollars—every cent of which was well earned. Some of them then

risked riding alone to Santa Fé, where they could
rest before signing contracts to guide more wagons.
Steve remembered that, shortly before leaving the
fort with the column, he had heard that a wagon
train was due. The Brogans must have heard of
this, too, and of the trail scout's plans.

Suddenly Steve forgot his fear in a burst of
fury.

"You're dead right I'd warn the scout if I saw
him!" he shouted. "That man, whoever he is,
guides and protects decent folk when they travel
wild territory and he deserves something better than
being shot in the back by a bunch of . . ."

An open hand flashed up. The flat of it slammed
against the side of Steve's face. Caught off balance,
he reeled and dropped to one knee. As he crouched,
a saddle boot prodded him in the ribs.

"Get up! We ain't finished with you yet . . . not
by a long way, we ain't."

Steve staggered to his feet, wondering whether to
try to break away. But in the same instant he knew
that any escape bid would be sure to fail. The moon
was giving good light and there was open ground all
round. He would certainly be shot down before
covering half a dozen paces.

One of the brothers inserted a forefinger through
the trigger guard of his ·44 Merwin Hulbert. He
began spinning the short-barrelled revolver like a
wheel. And he said casually: "We might as well fix
the kid now and be done with it. We don't want him
with us when this Catsfoot hombre comes along.

They do say Catsfoot's a hard number to handle and we want to give him our best attention."

Steve gave an uncontrollable gasp of astonishment.

Catsfoot . . . !

That trail scout was a living legend in the new territories. Pioneers gladly waited months to get places in his wagon trains, for it was said that men and their families were always safe when Catsfoot was in charge. In a strange way, he could sense danger when it was far off. And he always took the right measures to avoid it. His wagon trains never knew the horror of being encircled by hostile Indians. They never floundered uncertainly for days, their food running short, because the way had been lost. To Catsfoot, the safety of those under his care came before all else and he had the infinite skill to ensure that safety. His name was mentioned with love and respect by many men, women and children who had travelled far to help build a great new empire in the West. To them, during their journey into the unknown, he had been a torch and a shield.

Steve remembered that there was something else about Catsfoot which was also legendary. That was his guns. Catsfoot wore two of them and folks said that he could draw them with uncanny speed. But according to those stories, the only sure way of annoying that good-natured man was to speak of him as a gunfighter. For Catsfoot did not like using his guns and he looked forward to the time when they would no longer be necessary to protect himself and those under his care.

Like many other youngsters in the new territories, Steve had longed to set eyes on Catsfoot. He had dreamed of talking with him.

Now Steve thought: "I'm going to be killed . . . and I won't be able to warn Catsfoot. . . ."

In his imagination, he could see Catsfoot riding into the ambush set by the Brogans. Whatever his skill with his two guns, obviously he could do nothing to defend himself against bullets aimed at his back.

Abruptly, Steve realised that the Brogans had grouped themselves close round him. The one who had been spinning his gun had stopped doing so. That gun was being pressed against Steve's chest.

"This is it, bugle boy," a hard voice said. "We can't risk havin' you around. . . ."

Steve tried to twist away. But powerful hands grasped his wrists, so that he could scarcely move.

Eyes dilated with horror, he stared at the gun and at the hand which held it. He saw the forefinger move back the merest fraction, taking first pressure on the trigger. . . .

CHAPTER TWO

A MAN IN BUCKSKINS

STEVE told himself: "It'll be over in a second . . . mebbe I won't even feel any pain. . . ."

He knew that the trigger finger need move back only another tenth of an inch. Then the retaining ratchet would free the hammer and twenty-three grains of black powder would explode, despatching a lead bullet at a speed of a thousand feet a second.

But that finger did not move any further back.

Instead, it relaxed its pressure on the trigger. And slowly, very deliberately, the gun was taken away from Steve's chest.

At first, his numbed senses were unable to understand the reason. He wondered whether the end was being delayed to torture him.

Then he heard the hooves. . . .

He heard the distant and easy beating of them—the rhythm of a horse being ridden at a gentle canter. And the Brogans were muttering among themselves.

"That could be Catsfoot. . . !"

"Yep, that's almost certain. . . ."

"He's kind of early. We didn't expect him till to-morrow. . . ."

"We can't use the gun on the kid now, unless we want Catsfoot to have warnin'. . . ."

There was an iced silence. Then one of them said to Steve: "We're goin' to put you to sleep, kid, just so you don't get any ideas about yellin' out."

The man who had been holding the gun, quickly reversed the weapon until he was grasping it by the barrel. Then, using it like a bludgeon, he brought the butt down towards the top of Steve's head.

Instinctively, Steve jerked his head aside. At the same time, he threw himself back. He glimpsed the dark smudge of the revolver butt flashing close in front of his face. And he felt a jolt against his shoulders as he crashed against the man behind him—the Brogan who was gripping his wrists. That grip was momentarily relaxed. The moment was long enough for Steve to wrench his arms free. He tried to swivel round, intending to run—to run towards the approaching rider. But he had not taken the first step before a wildly swinging fist hit the back of his neck. He felt a tingling pain travel the length of his spine. In the ordinary way, he would have fallen and probably lost consciousness. But semi-hysterical desperation kept him on his feet. At the same time, he told himself: "I've got to shout. . . ."

The entire weight of one of the Brogans slammed against him like a flying boulder. Off balance, Steve spun on his heels. A huge hand was slapped over his open mouth. Other hands again held his arms, pulling them behind his back.

Now there was only one real freedom of move-

ment left to Steve—the use of his feet. So he
kicked. And immediately he felt the toe of his
cavalry boot jab hard against a shin bone. There
was a muffled grunt and a shadowy figure staggered
sideways, bent in pain.

That figure lurched against one of the three
horses.

The animal was already nervous because of the
struggle. Now it reared high, at the same time
giving a loud, frightened whinny.

But Steve was not aware of that. He had managed
to part his mouth. Twisting his head, he sank his
teeth into the hand which was silencing him. The
hand was snatched away. He took in a shallow,
panting breath and again tried to call out. Only a
faint croak came from his throat, like an episode in
a nightmare.

Something incredibly hard smashed against his
left cheekbone. He knew, even as his brain seemed
to explode, that it was the gun butt. The dim
figures of the Brogans swirled round him. Then
they vanished and he was looking through half-
closed eyelids at the moon. After the first shock, he
was not aware of pain. He knew only that the last of
his strength had gone. He could not struggle any
more. The odds had always been impossible. Now
his muscles and his mind were battered and
squeezed dry.

But the Brogans were not bothering about him :
not concerned to knock him completely insensible.
They had spaced themselves well apart. Their guns

out, they were staring towards the approaching
rider.

And those hoof beats were close now—very close.

They were no longer cantering. The rhythm had
gone. It was as if the horse was moving uncertainly,
its owner suspecting danger but far from sure.

Steve heard one of the Brogans whisper: "We'll
take him just as soon as he gets in sight—don't give
him a chance to draw!"

Suddenly Steve saw it; saw the horse. It towered
above him in the half-light. But the Brogans did not
fire. For a moment, Steve could not understand
why. Then he saw the reason. The saddle was
empty.

The animal stopped a few yards away, ears
twitching. From the Brogans came a puzzled, confused muttering. One of them began moving
towards the horse.

But he did not get far. Not more than a couple of
paces. A voice stopped him. It was a quiet, clear
voice. The words came slowly, almost casually. But
their meaning was lethal.

That voice said: "You'll all keep nice and still and
don't let anyone try turning round. . . ."

It came from behind the Brogans and near to
them. It seemed to solidify them. They became as
still as slabs of stone.

Steve wondered whether his mind had collapsed
under strain and he was dreaming it all. Still
sprawled on the ground, he twisted round.

He saw a man in buckskins, a man who was very

tall and slender. His fair hair came down to his shoulders and the moonlight, which was full on his face, showed fine, almost delicate features. It could be the face of a painter or a poet—except for one fact. Except that at this moment there was an iron hard set about the jaw and the blue eyes were as cold and relentless as the blue steel of the guns he was holding.

Those guns . . . they were the latest Colt model—the ·45 double-action Peacemakers. The one in the left hand was slightly advanced and at nearly shoulder height. The other was level with the waist. Each of those guns was moving in slow, small circles so that arms and wrists were kept supple for instant action.

Steve knew that this was Catsfoot. It had to be Catsfoot. There was something about the way he held those Colts which had the stamp of genius. Something relaxed yet alert, which spoke of a man who had brought gun play to an exact science. Here was the trail scout who was said to be able to draw as fast—or perhaps even faster—than the Brogans.

Steve's brain cleared and his bruised body gained strength. And he felt a thrill of excitement as he realised that Catsfoot was speaking to him, without taking his eyes off the Brogans. Now his tones were gentle, friendly. He was saying: "Sorry I couldn't interfere sooner, son. You hurt bad?"

"I'll be okay."

"You must have been with Lieutenant Anderson's

column. I heard about it leaving the fort just before I arrived there. Any other survivors?"

Steve shook his head as he got shakily to his feet. "They were all cut down—didn't have a chance."

"How come I find you taking a beating from these three big critters? Who are they?"

"They're the Brogan brothers," Steve said, moving closer to Catsfoot. "They were waiting for you—figured you must have money. . . ."

In a few sentences, Steve filled in the details. And as he listened, Catsfoot's face became tauter, harder. He told Steve: "I'm going to have a talk with these hombres and I don't want to run any risk of you being hurt, so keep well away from me, son."

Reluctantly, Steve moved a few paces away. The Brogans, still with their backs to Catsfoot and still holding their guns, remained as still as statues.

Catsfoot told them: "Drop your guns—then you can turn round."

But the Brogans kept their guns in their hands. Neither did they turn. They remained utterly motionless.

"Mebbe you didn't hear me right," Catsfoot said quietly. "I told you to drop your artillery and face me."

There was a long, strained silence. Catsfoot broke it.

"Up to now, I've never shot anyone in the back," he said. "But there could be a first time. I could give you what you were planning for me—so don't push me too far."

After a moment of silence there was a soft thud.

One of the Brogans had dropped his gun on to the sage. Then another gun fell from reluctant fingers. Two of them had disarmed themselves and they turned to face Catsfoot.

That was the moment of sudden crisis—the single second in which several events happened at brain-shattering speed.

One of the Brogans still retained his gun. He was the cause of it. This man also swung round, making his move the merest fraction after the others. When he completed his turn, he threw himself bodily to one side. As he hurtled through the air, he fired.

Catsfoot was moving, too. Moving to his left with the irresistible speed of an uncoiling spring.

Three explosions came together, blending into an ugly symphony—one from a ·44 Merwin Hulbert, the two others created by a pair of ·45 Colt Peacemakers. And the scene was lighted by their searing flashes.

Then the moment was over. . . .

Catsfoot was bending slightly forward. Under the moonlight, thin trails of smoke could be seen rising from his rock-steady guns. Ten yards from him, the figure of one of the Brogans lay twisting and moaning.

Dropping his guns into their holsters, Catsfoot moved until he was standing over the man.

"You're wounded in the legs," he said. "But you're not going to die—yet. I aim to take all of you

Catsfoot moved with the speed of an uncoiling spring.

right back to the fort with me. I guess it's time you stood trial."

The wounded man glared up, his eyes wild in the sickly light.

"It's a long ride back to Fort Coulter, Catsfoot. You'll never get us there! Mebbe you're lookin' smart right now, but me and m'brothers will fix you if you try handin' us over to the law!"

"I'll take that chance," Catsfoot said. "There's going to be a lot of . . . *Hold it!*"

The last two words came like the double crack of a whip. And as he uttered them, his guns came out. They seemed to jump up into his hands. The double movement was completed faster than the brain could think, a supreme example of natural genius, allied to a close study of bone and muscle structure, plus years of continuous practice.

Catsfoot's Peacemakers were levelled at the two other brothers. They had eased their stance very slightly. Each of them was partly bent forward. Each was on the point of snatching his Merwin Hulbert from the ground, fingers within inches of the butts.

"I had a hunch you might try that," Catsfoot said. "Now take a couple of steps back."

Slowly, the Brogans straightened then moved away from their guns.

Then Catsfoot said to Steve: "You can keep one of those shooting irons, son. Throw the others in the river."

First Steve picked up the gun which had belonged

to the wounded man. This he pushed under his tunic belt. Then, keeping a careful eye on the two glowering Brogans, he took the guns which lay on the sage. Holding one in each hand, he walked quickly towards the river, picking his way between the chilling relics of the massacre. He slithered down the slope, until almost at the water's edge. For a short time, he paused there, the guns still in his hands, looking at the reflection of the moon and thinking.

It seemed incredible that, little more than two days before, he had ridden out of Fort Coulter with a standing patrol of fifty troopers. Now only he was left alive. And, as he considered it, he realised that the arrival of the Brogans was the sort of thing which could have been expected; for white outlaws often moved in after battles between soldiers and Apaches, in the hope of picking up discarded loot. As well as being traitors to their own people, they were human vultures. The Brogans must have counted it a stroke of good fortune to be able to ferret among the battle casualties while waiting to ambush Catsfoot. Steve pondered on the quirk of fate which had enabled him and Catsfoot to save each other's lives. For Catsfoot, with the acute hearing of a trail scout, had certainly been warned by the sound of the struggle with the Brogans. And his arrival from the rear had prevented Steve being killed later. Now the question was whether Catsfoot would be able to get the Brogans to Fort Coulter. Although now unarmed, it was obvious that they would take a risk to avoid a trial and certain hanging if delivered to the army.

Abruptly, Steve realised that in standing here and brooding, he was wasting time. And he gave a brief shiver as a cool breeze penetrated his still-wet uniform. He tossed the two Merwin Hulberts into the water, then turned and scrambled up the bank.

It was when he reached the top of it that he halted in mid-stride.

He heard a cough.

It was a feeble, retching sound coming from a few yards to his left. For a moment, Steve wondered whether it was the croak of some animal. Then it was repeated. It was unmistakably human.

Steve fumbled for the gun under his belt. He drew it and cocked the hammer, at the same time wondering whether to call out to Catsfoot. He decided against that for two reasons. One was that to do so would reveal his presence and position to whoever was there, the other that Catsfoot was fully occupied watching the Brogans.

Very cautiously, Steve moved towards the locality of the sound. After a few steps, he stopped. That man—for a man it surely must be—should now be easily within sight. But only moonlit space surrounded him. Steve turned a circle, keeping the gun waist high. Still nothing.

He thought: "Mebbe I've made a mistake after all. It . . ."

A soft hissing reached him. It stopped, then started again, only to be broken by that cough.

Steve looked at the ground. Two feet ahead of him, a long dark object lay partly concealed by the sagebrush. He dropped to his knees, then gave a choking sob. Dull, pain-racked eyes were staring at him out of a grey, blood-smeared face.

It was the face of Lieutenant Anderson.

Now Steve did not hesitate. He shouted for Catsfoot.

Catsfoot completed a quick examination.

"He's got a deep bullet wound in the middle of his chest," he said, getting to his feet. "He should be dead—I guess he looked dead enough for the Apaches to leave him alone."

Steve reminded himself that another reason why the lieutenant still lived was because the Apaches did not normally scalp battle victims—unlike the Oglallas, Brulés, and other Sioux tribes, or the Cheyenne and Kiowas of the mid-western plains.

The Apaches—although by far the most ruthless and warlike of all the Indian races—seldom mutilated the dead.

Steve whispered to Catsfoot: "He seems to be conscious . . . has he any chance?"

"I don't know for sure, but I've stopped the worst of the bleeding. Anyway, we've got to get him to a doctor, and fast."

"But the nearest doctor's at the fort!" Steve said.

"I know that—and we can't take him there. He'd never stand the journey."

Steve asked desperately: "Then what *are* we to do? We can't let him stay here and die!"

Catsfoot pushed his fedora back from his forehead. "There's a small canyon just a few miles from here. Mebbe we can get him there, where there's plenty of good shelter in the caves. You'll have to look after him while I ride to the fort."

Steve nodded. He knew the canyon. Although narrow and a bare three hundred yards long, its rock walls were pitted with caves. There was a stream for drinking water, and sun-dried cactus to light fires against the chill of the night. Then Steve remembered the Brogans. The wounded brother had been brought along by the two others. Now all three were sitting on the ground, close enough to be well within sight, but too far away to rush Catsfoot.

"I guess we'll have to let them go," Steve said.

"There's nothing else for it, son." Then, raising his voice, Catsfoot said to the Brogans: "I was hoping to see you all stand trial in the next few days, but I guess that'll have to wait."

A grating laugh went up from the Brogans. But it faded when they heard Catsfoot tell Steve: "Bring my horse over here—and you'll need one of theirs for yourself."

One of the brothers shouted: "You can't leave us a hoss short—not in this territory!"

"I've got more to worry about than your comfort," Catsfoot said evenly.

"But we ain't got our guns, neither! We're defenceless!"

"Mebbe that's not such a bad thing. Anyway, it looks like you have plenty of friends among the Apaches, so mebbe they'll fix you up."

Meantime, Steve found Catsfoot's horse, which had wandered a short distance upriver in search of soft grass to crop. Then he selected the most powerful of the Brogans' animals and checked its saddle bag. He was pleased to find it well filled with pemmican biscuits. There was also a bag of coffee beans and chicory. That, plus some of the hard tack which Catsfoot had with him, meant that there would be enough food to feed Anderson for several days.

Steve returned leading the two horses. Catsfoot said: "I'm going to be busy for the next minute . . . if any of the Brogans move an inch, use that gun of yours."

Steve pulled the Merwin Hulbert from his belt, levelled it at the three men. Catsfoot again bent over Anderson. Very gently, he inserted one arm under the lieutenant's shoulders, the other behind his knees. The taut strength in Catsfoot's tall and slender body was shown by the effortless way he lifted the heavy burden and walked towards his horse. He placed Anderson in the saddle and supported the limp figure with one hand, then vaulted behind him. The horse shuffled and stamped the ground, as if in protest against the double weight. That Anderson was at least partly conscious was made clear by his partly open eyes. But he was too weak even to speak or to hold himself upright. Catsfoot's left arm, now circled round Anderson's chest, took the entire strain. His other hand held the reins.

"Get mounted," he said to Steve, "but keep your gun ready."

Still holding the Merwin Hulbert, Steve swung into the saddle. There was a faint movement from two of the Brogans. There was nothing distinct about it, nothing even menacing. It was as if they were merely preparing to take a chance, if a chance should come. But Catsfoot's voice cut at them.

"Don't get any tough ideas," he said. "I can still reach for my right hand gun if I have to . . . !" He paused, letting the warning take effect. Then he said to Steve: "Come on, son. We can only move slow, but I want to reach the canyon before daylight."

They turned towards the south and away from the river, at no more than an easy trot. But even at that pace, Catsfoot had trouble keeping Anderson in the saddle. The lieutenant's body rolled loosely, like that of a broken doll. He slipped to one side, then the other. Several times he groaned.

They had covered less than thirty yards when the voice of one of the Brogans came to them. It came clearly and heavy with hate.

"We'll fix you for this, Catsfoot!" it shouted. "Mebbe we'll have to follow you to the other end of the territory, but that don't matter none. We'll find you when you ain't expectin' us . . . and we'll fix you good . . ."

The moon had set and they had ridden through a period of utter blackness. A period when the wind had a biting chill as it moaned in the sage. It was as though they were the only living things in a lonely and condemned world.

But now dawn was smudging the low sky. And ahead, very close, they could see jagged, forbidding shadows. They were the rocks of the canyon. Thousands of years before when the ice melted, those rocks had been deposited in short and ugly parallel lines. And the same mighty cataclysm had torn bare what had been an underground stream. In the succeeding ages, the stream had sunk deeper and deeper, till now the walls of the canyon were never less than six hundred feet high, almost vertical, unscalable by man or beast. A place only for vultures, of which there were many.

But the base of the canyon was different. For a few yards on each side of the stream there grew stringy grass, soapweed and, farther back, the yellow-flowered Prickly Pear cactus. There, too, were the caves, some of them mere hollows in the red rock. Others went far back—deep, forbidding tunnels. There the cougar, the jaguar, and the coyote sometimes sought shelter.

There was only one narrow entrance to the canyon—at the north end. The other extremity was blocked by massive deposits of rock, as high as those on each side.

Steve shivered as they rode into the place. Partly it was because of the wind cutting through his damp uniform. Partly through a sudden sense of fear which he could not explain. It was as though they were riding into the narrow gates of a vast prison.

Catsfoot glanced at him and said: "You'll have to get those clothes off just as soon as the sun's up."

"I'm all right," Steve told him without much conviction. "This canyon . . . it's a strange sort of place in the half-light. Full of shadows. I came here with a patrol a few months ago, but that was in full day then . . . it wasn't like this."

Catsfoot laughed softly. "Shadows don't hurt, Steve. There's good shelter here and that's what we need for Anderson while I ride to the fort."

They were now through the narrow parting of rock at the entrance and well inside the canyon. To their right, the stream bubbled, looking like ink in the murk, and on each side, were those towering walls.

"If I remember, there's a good cave around this spot," Catsfoot said. They took their horses across the stream. Catsfoot's arms were firmly linked round Anderson's waist. The slumped body must have drained his strength, but he did not show it. Twice during the ride, Catsfoot had halted to examine the lieutenant. The bleeding, although it continued, was no longer serious. And he was still alive. That was the best that could be said for him. He was now completely unconscious.

On the other side of the stream they reined in. Steve dismounted and supported Anderson while Catsfoot got out of the saddle. For a few moments Catsfoot rubbed his arms.

Abruptly, he ceased doing so.

He became as tense as a cougar about to spring. He was staring towards the far end of the canyon.

And suddenly the day came, the half-light became a subdued radiance.

It showed people huddled round the stream. Tattered, worn, pitiable people. Men, most of them, but a few women were there and children. They were flat on their stomachs like animals, sucking up the water. About them was the appearance of utter despair, of absolute defeat.

And they were whites.

CHAPTER THREE

PAWNS OF THE APACHES

THERE are moments when the coolest brain becomes paralysed. Moments when the mind is a pulp, when bone and muscle are putty.

For Catsfoot and Steve, this was such a moment. They saw clearly, but at first they did not accept the evidence of their eyes.

Then gradually, they absorbed the ghastly details. In all, there were about forty of those whites. They must have been living in the caves at the distant end of the canyon, for on the rocks outside them were stretched what seemed to be washed clothing—a few torn shirts, women's blouses, and a child's jerkin. . . .

When they had drunk from the stream, they returned to the caves in ones and twos. They walked slowly, reeling slightly, like figments of a nightmare. And when they reached the caves, they sprawled in the openings, motionless, staring at nothing. None of them had so far noticed Catsfoot and Steve.

It was Steve who broke the ghastly silence. He whispered: "Who are they . . . why are they here?"

By now Catsfoot had fully recovered. But a

pallor in his face showed the shock he had received.

"We'll know soon enough—first we've got to get the lieutenant under shelter."

He lifted Anderson from the saddle. Gently, he laid him just within the cave which was a few yards from them. Then he said: "Now we'll talk to these folk."

Slowly, they walked along the bank of the stream, which flowed into an underground cavern at the other end of the canyon. They had covered less than a hundred yards when they saw some of that strange huddle of people get unsteadily to their feet. And, as the distance narrowed, they saw, too, that hunger was written on all of their faces. They were drawn, grey faces, the eyes unnaturally large.

A red-bearded man, wearing ragged canvas breeches and nothing else, took a few tottering steps towards them. He eyed them in dim disbelief. In a voice which was cracked and shrill, he said to Catsfoot: "They have let y'keep y'guns and hosses . . . why do they let y'do that? But they'll have 'em off you soon. You see . . . they'll soon take those . . ."

When only a few feet separated them, Catsfoot stopped. He said quietly: "No one'll take my guns or my horse from me if I can do anything about it, stranger. Now mebbe you'll tell me who you all are and why you're livin' like this?"

The bearded man rubbed his emaciated chest. He did not appear to hear. Or, if he heard, not to understand.

Catsfoot repeated the question. This time, the man lowered himself on to a boulder, as though weary of the strain of standing. He said: "Y'mean y'just rode into this canyon? You . . . you weren't brought here?"

"We rode in because we wanted to—me, the boy, and a wounded cavalry officer."

For a time the man was silent, taking in the words. By now, some of the others had approached, staring at Catsfoot and Steve as if doubting their reality.

Then the man said: "The Apaches brought us to this canyon. We're—we're what's left of a wagon train that left Chimney Butte for Tucson . . . the Apaches took us mebbe six weeks ago. They brought us here and here—here we've stayed."

"But there're no Apaches in the canyon! Why don't you get out? Anything's better than staying right here and starving."

The bearded man gave a laugh. It was shrill, humourless.

"They find you if you try to get out, mister! A man don't get far without a hoss. Two of us tried to make a break. They were brought back and the Apaches killed 'em right here in front of us. But that ain't all . . . no sir, that ain't all. They picked two more of us out and knifed them, as well. And they said they'd go right on doin' that every time any of us tried to reach the fort for help. They let us have a bit of food, mister. Every noontime, some of 'em ride in and leave us some meat and pemmican . . . just enough to keep us alive and no more."

"And why are you being held here?"

"Don't know for sure . . . as hostages, I guess."

Catsfoot nodded slowly. That they were hostages was almost certainly the answer. The Apaches were skilled, ruthless tacticians. They sometimes preserved white captives unharmed—provided they were not soldiers—so that they could be used for bargaining with United States authorities. Many times they had saved themselves from encirclement and defeat by threatening to massacre prisoners. Even more often, they had secured the release of their own captured braves in exchange for a few whites.

But here, in this canyon, was a difference. Here were many captives, all seized at the same time, held like animals, for barter or slaughter.

Suddenly Catsfoot asked: "You say you were all in a wagon train from Chimney Butte for Tucson—who was your scout?"

"A hombre by name of Housler."

"Which trail did he use?"

"We skirted east of the Mogollon Mesa."

"Then . . . ?"

"Then he reckoned to fasten on the Rio Verde till we hit the Casa Grande Trail. That was fastest, he told us."

Catsfoot muttered something under his breath. But aloud he said: "That was just murder. There're a whole lot too many trail scouts around who don't know their work—or run risks to collect fast dollars. I guess I'm telling you something you've already learned, but the Casa Grande's thick with Apaches' lodges. It's one of their big hunting territories. There's only one safe trail and that's to swing way out west over Cactus Plain and to come into Tucson by way of Hot Springs and Phoenix."

The bearded man said: "Y'right, mister. But it ain't no use blamin' that scout now—he died when the Apaches attacked."

"I'm sorry about that, but I guess a lot of other folk died, too, just because he was stupid."

There was a thoughtful silence. Then the bearded man said: "You seem to know a whole lot about it, mister. Who are you?"

"Folks call me Catsfoot."

That crowd of starved, haggard people reacted in different ways. Some got uncertainly to their feet. Others, who had been listening to the talk in a disinterested way, suddenly looked up. A few repeated the name under their breaths. But in every face there was one factor in common—the flickering birth of hope.

"You're . . . you're the trail scout and gun fighter," the bearded man croaked.

"I'm a trail scout. I use guns when I have to. But that doesn't make me a gun fighter," Catsfoot said, an edge to his voice.

"I'm sorry, Catsfoot . . . it's just that word gets around . . ." He broke off and put out a thin and shaking hand. "I'm Luke Vachell. I was a head teamster with the wagon train."

Smiling, Catsfoot took his hand.

By now, all the captives were gathered close around him. Each calling out his own name, each striving to make himself known to the slender trail scout in buckskins who towered above them. One of the last to approach was a quiet little man, wearing the torn remnants of city clothes. Rimless spectacles, one lens cracked, clung to his snub nose.

"I'm Doc Fulton," he said with an attempt at cheerfulness.

"Doc . . . you're a doctor?"

"Sure am. But I ain't got any drugs or instruments for my trade right now. Apaches took them."

Catsfoot gripped his arm.

"We've got a wounded officer in that cave by the entrance. Wounded bad. I want you to go to him. See what you can do."

Doc Fulton hesitated. Then he said: "Bullet wound?"

"Sure is."

"Bullet still there?"

"Deep in the chest."

"Then it doesn't look so good, but I'll see if I can get it out . . . loan me your knife, Catsfoot."

Catsfoot pulled the blade from its scabbard. It was thin and as flexible as the stock end of a whip. Doc Fulton tested the cutting edge. "Sharper than many a scalpel," he said. "Guess this'll do."

"You'd better have some help," Catsfoot said, "I'll . . ."

"I'll manage on my own," the doctor told him, shaking his head till his spectacles wobbled. Then, despite his weakness, he moved briskly towards the other end of the canyon.

Catsfoot turned again to Luke. "Are you in charge here?"

Luke shook his head. "The Apaches are in charge—no one else."

"You all seem to have given up hope."

"Anyone would give up hope after weeks without enough to eat and bottled up in this place, just waitin' . . . waitin' to know whether you're goin' to die."

"Mebbe that's so. But from now on we're going to organise. All of you are going to get out of this canyon. And you're going to reach safety—get it?"

They stared at Catsfoot with doubtful interest, wanting to believe him, scarcely daring to do so.

Luke said: "I figure that just ain't possible. Mebbe *you* can get away. You've got a hoss and you're armed. Same with this kid. But what chance have *we* got?"

Catsfoot sat on a stone beside Luke. The others clustered round him. And they listened intently as he spoke in his quiet, clear way.

"First," he said, "I've got to have facts. You say some Apaches ride here every noontime with food. How many of them?"

"Mebbe a dozen," Luke answered. "Sometimes a few more, sometimes less."

"What do they do—do all of them ride right up to this end of the canyon?"

"Yep, they know they have nothing to be scared of—not from us. If any one of us tries to start any trouble, they're certain to kill him and mebbe a couple more of us as well. Them that come in here always have good guns, too. Anyway, we ain't got the strength to do anything. Not on the chickenfeed chuck they give us."

Catsfoot's blue eyes were thoughtful. He asked: "Do you know if there are any more Apaches waiting outside the canyon?"

"Can't be sure about that, but I figure not."

"I'll soon know for certain," Catsfoot said. "Stay right where you are. I'll be back in a few minutes . . ."

He beckoned to Steve. Together they strode towards the narrow entrance. They paused at the cave where they had left Anderson. The doctor was holding the lieutenant's pulse. He looked up and said: "I got the slug out. Lucky he's unconscious. Awake, he'd never have stood the pain."

"Is he going to . . . ?"

Doc Fulton shrugged. "If I had drugs I'd say he'd a good chance. But I've got nothing except your knife. And I've had to use what's left of my shirt for bandages. But this soldier's tough. He *must* be tough or he'd have died hours ago. So I say he's on even odds."

"Are you going to keep him there?"

"Yep. Can't risk moving him any more. I'll stay with him the rest of the day. Then I'll ask for volunteers for the night."

Catsfoot said: "You're doing a fine job, doc." Then they passed their horses, which were cropping the thin grass at the water edge, splashed through the stream and passed between the towering cliffs out of the canyon. There Catsfoot made a careful examination of the ground. He walked in widening circles, body bent slightly forward.

Then he straightened and returned to Steve, who was waiting just inside the entrance.

"What d'you think?" Steve asked.

"The earth's rocky round here and that doesn't make it easy. But there's heavy spoors of unshod ponies coming in here from the north-east—the sort of tracks they'd make if they were using the same route every day. Right outside the canyon, the tracks get heavier and narrow and there's no sign of any others. That looks to me as if all of them come in—which is what I want."

Steve wanted to ask Catsfoot about his plan. But he knew it was best to be patient. He would know at the same time as the others.

They returned to the far end of the canyon. There the hostages were waiting, exactly as they had left them, save that the smaller children were now playing at the side of the stream. Catsfoot told them of what he had seen. Then, raising his voice slightly, he said: "At around high noon to-day,

some Apaches will ride in here. But forget the
Apaches for a minute. Just think about their
horses and guns."

Luke again rubbed his bare chest. "That don't
mean anything to us," he said. "Them Apaches
ain't goin' to hand us their hosses or their guns."

"I figure we can take them," Catsfoot said
slowly.

There was a brief moment of quiet. Then a rush
of voices.

"That ain't possible. . . ."

"Mebbe you could kill one or two . . ."

"Yep, then they'd slay half a dozen of us . . ."

Luke summed it up. Raising a thin hand for
silence, he said to Catsfoot: "We all respect you,
mister. We all know a lot about you and all we know
is good. But we've got just one hope of survivin'
and that's the chance of bein' traded in exchange for
Injun prisoners. We'll stick to that chance. We
don't aim to throw our lives away on some scarum
scheme that don't have a chance of workin'."

Catsfoot pushed back his fedora, his lips turned
in a half-smile.

"It's no scarum scheme that I've got in my mind.
I can't make you do anything you don't want to do
and I don't aim to try. But mebbe you'll listen to
me before deciding."

Luke said reluctantly: "Okay, Catsfoot, we'll
listen."

Catsfoot paused, collecting his thoughts. He
knew that to these direct and simple people, whose

morale was naturally low, he must be careful to make
every point doubly clear.

"Let me start with a piece of personal history,"
he began. "You folks say you know a lot about me.
Mebbe you know I was scout with the Union armies
in the Civil War. I had nearly four years of it and in
that time a man can learn a lot about tactics—
military tactics. If we use some of that knowledge,
I figure we've taken the first step to being free. . . ."

He stopped, looked around, then asked: "Do you
know the fastest way to win any battle, big or small?
Mebbe you don't, but if he was well enough, the
lieutenant would support what I'm telling you. It's
to encircle the enemy. Cut them off from their base.
Then draw the circle tight, so they've no room to
manoeuvre. Put them under fire from every angle."

Luke said: "There's nothin' new about that.
Them's the tactics the Apaches use."

"You're right—and the Apaches are good tacticians. Do you think a handful of them would think
of riding into this canyon if they thought you had
even one gun among you? They would not. Once
inside this canyon, they could be prevented from
ever getting out. Just one man in that narrow pass,
hidden by the rocks, could pick them all off."

There was a stir of interest—interest tempered
with fear.

Luke said: "There's your guns. And I see the
kid's gotta gun under his belt."

"That's what I mean, Luke."

"You figure on hiding in the entrance and pickin'

them off when they all get inside? Well . . . mebbe
it can be done. But you've forgotten just two facts,
Catsfoot."

"Tell me about them."

"First, some of us folks stand a mighty big chance
of being killed before the last Apache dies. Second,
them Apaches think and move fast. I guess some of
'em will be behind cover before you can hit 'em.
Then what happens? You can't move and mebbe
they can't, either. But to-morrow at the latest, more
of them Injuns'll be along to see what's happening."
He shook his head and added: "Nope, I don't think
it figures."

Catsfoot said very softly: "I'll make a promise to
all of you—I'll get every one of those Apaches
before they can raise their rifles."

"No man can promise that. I have heard you're
a mighty fast gun, but this is talkin' too big."

"I'm not talking big, Luke. I don't like big
talkers. I'm just telling you what I feel I can do."

"Yep, but no man can shoot as straight and as fast
as that."

"Some men can. I figure I'm one of them."

Suddenly one of the women shouted: "We ain't
goin' to be killed just 'cause you think you're a top
gun!"

There was a growl of agreement. And an old
prospector, his eyes pouched and dim, staggered
forward. He said: "In m'time I've seen a lot of
gun-slingers. I've seen Jesse James, Billy the Kid,
Cole Younger . . . I've seen 'em draw and shoot.

Mebbe Billy *might* be able to do what you're thinkin' of. Yep, mebbe Billy the Kid, if he had a lot of luck. But no one else. Not even you, Catsfoot!"

Catsfoot gave a heavy sigh. Then he said: "I don't want to do this, but it looks like I've got to prove something. First, take those children into the caves. I don't want to have them scared . . ."

Someone rounded up the children from the stream and ushered them away. The rest watched Catsfoot silently, doubtfully.

Then Catsfoot said to the old-timer: "I've seen Billy the Kid pull a gun, too. You're right about him—he's fast. Very fast. But now I want you to do some comparing. You got a silver dollar in your breeches?"

"Sure I have."

"Take it out."

The old timer produced the coin.

"Now stand well clear of the others."

Still clutching the dollar, he stumbled towards a bare piece of cliff.

Catsfoot moved away till about twenty paces separated the two men. Then Catsfoot called: "Hold that dollar out sideways, shoulder high and let it drop any time you like."

The old-timer's face quivered.

"Hey! I don't wanta be filled with your slugs!"

"You won't! Are you going to do like I say—or do I have to shoot the coin out of your fingers?"

"I . . . aw, heck, I guess I'm goin' to be killed anyhow . . ."

Unwillingly, he raised his arms. Catsfoot watched him, that left foot slightly forward, hands hanging at his side. Relaxed, almost indifferent.

The old-timer's fingers parted.

Steve saw them part. He saw the coin begin to fall. Then something happened to that coin. It began to dance in the air. It flew ten feet up. Then it jerked to one side and the other. It dropped to within inches of the ground, before swerving up again at an acute angle. And while it was in the middle of its flashing flight it seemed to stop, to come to a trembling standstill in mid-air. And, through every fantastic second, the eardrums trembled under the impact of reverberating explosions.

The last explosion blew the coin to pieces. The jagged bits fell at the old-timer's feet.

Catsfoot ejected twelve empty shells from his Peacemakers. He was re-loading them as he strolled back to the old-timer.

"Could Billy have beaten that?" he asked.

The old-timer was blinking at the pieces of coin. He shook his head. "I figure even Billy couldn't have done that," he mumbled.

The others, too, were staring at the remnants on the ground. Someone said: "I wouldn't like to quarrel with you, Catsfoot."

"No particular reason why you shouldn't if you feel that way," Catsfoot told him. "I don't use my guns unless someone draws on me first ... or unless I have to help folks."

Luke took the hint. He said: "I guess this proves it. If anyone can even the score with them Apaches, you can. I don't know about the rest, but I've changed my mind. I'm for lettin' you try your idea."

There was a mumble of agreement, which suddenly faded.

"Hey, Catsfoot!"

The interruption came from the old-timer. He was shaking with indignation.

"Hey . . . that was my silver dollar you blowed to bits! You owe me money, mister!"

Smiling, Catsfoot passed over a coin. All the others were smiling, too. But they faded when Luke shouted: "We've all been forgettin' one big fact, Catsfoot. Suppose you fix them Injuns—what happens then? We'll have mebbe a dozen hosses and the same number of guns. But there're forty-one people here, countin' the kids. Those who get a hoss stand a chance of reachin' Fort Coulter. But what about those who don't have hosses? They'll be worse off than now. And there's a wounded army officer in that far cave—what'll y'do about him?"

Catsfoot said: "I figure we can all reach the fort. Less than a dozen horses'll be enough. Now listen. . . ."

High noon. . . .

The canyon was an open oven. The sun concentrated its savagery within the tall, gaunt walls. The rocks were hot to the touch, the air seemed to scorch the lungs. Even the cacti looked as if they might wilt and wither. This climax of heat lasted only for the hour when the sun was directly overhead. But for the hostages, it was a daily hour of torture.

They spent it within the shelter of their caves, mopping rivulets of sweat from their bodies. And waiting for the party of Apaches who brought the meagre rations to keep a flicker of life in their wasted frames.

They were all in one large cave now—waiting as they had so often waited.

But to-day there was a difference. . . .

Eyes, usually dull and flat under the burden of despair, were now bright with expectancy. Bodies which had been weak because of hunger, had suddenly found strength. But there was tension there, too. An acute anxiety which twisted the stomach into a hard knot, which made each breath a shallow, panting and briefly painful episode.

When they spoke, it was in grating whispers. They sought to reassure themselves by the sound of their voices; they hoped to be given protection from the pain of fear.

A mule skinner who had the shoulders of a steer and the round face of a good-natured child, said: "I'm thinkin' what'll happen to us if just one of them Apaches gets away . . ."

A little man who had been going to Tucson to take a job as an assay office clerk, nodded and said: "We'll all be dead before the day's out if Catsfoot misses . . ."

"But I don't figure he *can* miss—not the way he shoots. Not unless somethin' unexpected happens . . . mebbe the unexpected will happen. Y'never can be sure of . . ."

Luke interrupted. Luke was nursing the ·44 Merwin Hulbert. Steve had passed it to him on Catsfoot's orders. And Luke snarled: "You snivel like a bunch of old women! Nothin' will go wrong if y'keep your nerve. Nothin' at all! Understand? And just suppose Catsfoot does miss, and one of 'em comes at us? Ain't I got a gun, too? I'll be able to handle that kinda emergency, so take it easy!"

They became silent, glad of Luke's insults. Glad of the extra confidence they gave to them. And Steve, sitting close to Luke, admired the head teamster's newly-found faith in Catsfoot. Yet he could not help wondering whether Luke would be as accurate with the gun as he claimed, if an emergency really came.

But abruptly Steve ceased to wonder. He became even more strained, more intense. So did all the others.

They heard the howl of a coyote. Long and mournful. It was repeated three times. It came from the canyon entrance. They knew what it meant. It was the signal from Catsfoot for them to be ready. The Apaches were in sight.

CHAPTER FOUR

FURY AT NOON

No MORE than two horsemen could pass in or out of the canyon at one time. That was because the narrow space between the towering walls was made yet narrower by boulders scattered at each side. Catsfoot was crouched behind one of those boulders. By raising his head a few inches, he could gain a clear view of almost all the canyon. But at this moment he was entirely under cover—for the Apaches were riding in. And he could easily count their numbers by the sound of the unshod hoofs as they passed close to him.

Three . . . four . . . five. . . .

There was a gap between the riders, indicated by a brief, comparative silence.

Six . . . seven. . . .

That was the last of them. All were in the canyon now. Only seven! Fewer than he had expected. This was a stroke of luck which Catsfoot had not dared to hope for. But, even so, the odds were heavily against him. For, no matter how fast and accurate his shooting, there was always a strong possibility that at least one of the braves might succeed in taking cover behind a rock. If that happened, it might prove impossible to dislodge him. Then the result would be that the hostages would not be able to get out of the canyon, and Catsfoot would not be able to get into it.

Now Catsfoot looked cautiously over the boulder. At the same time, he laid in front of him six ·45 centre-fire cartridges, ready for a fast reload. He felt glad that his guns, only recently purchased, were the new Peacemaker models. These were the first double-action guns to be produced by Samuel Colt's firm. Other guns needed a flick back of the thumb to cock the hammer after each shot. But the Peacemakers had a device by which the hammers were cocked automatically by trigger pressure. That meant a faster rate of fire and greater accuracy.

The Apaches were now all within the canyon. They were riding slowly and in single file, keeping to the centre and close to the edge of the stream. The leader was level with the cave where Doc Fulton was tending Lieutenant Anderson. But there was little danger of their being discovered at the moment, for they had withdrawn deep into the shadows. And the horses belonging to Catsfoot and Steve had been hidden in another cave.

With surprising deliberation, Catsfoot lifted his guns from their holsters. He braced his back against the cliff face. Sweat was oozing down his face and through his buckskins. He was not only aware that this was a difficult task which he faced—a task out of which failure would certainly mean a hideous death for all the whites in the canyon. It was also heavily on his mind that, now the moment had come, he detested the thought of opening fire on unsuspecting men. The laws of war and the laws of logic told him that he should have no such qualm. The Apaches had not hesitated to slay many harmless members of the wagon train, and to subject the others to great suffering. Still he disliked it. But now there could be no retreat, no second thoughts.

With his left-hand gun, he drew a careful bead on one of the rearmost Apaches. Gently, he squeezed the trigger . . .

The trigger ratchet pressed down on the cylinder stop. The revolving cylinder forced back the hammer. Then the hammer fell as a cartridge aligned itself with the barrel.

In the confined space, the explosion seemed to repeat itself in a score of different places, each echo a crash of thunder.

There was nothing dramatic about the way that Apache fell. He simply rolled forward across his pony's neck, dropping at its feet.

And Catsfoot waited, waited for the crucial seconds when, the first shock overcome, the Apaches scattered.

This was the first move towards forcing the Apaches to disperse. And disperse they must, for while in single file and directly ahead of Catsfoot, they offered a strictly limited target.

There was not long to wait. For a weird moment the Apaches became motionless. They sat their ponies like castings of bronze. Then, as though struck by the power of a fantastic storm, they broke

The Apache rolled forward across his pony's neck.

column. Some lashed their ponies towards the far end of the canyon, where the hostages were under cover. Others galloped for the caves on either side.

Now Catsfoot had moved slightly forward. He was pivoting most of his weight on his right heel, so as to be able to turn easily. And he set about a careful tactic of "boxing in." Two of the remaining six Apaches were making for the distant end of the canyon. A slug fired from something over forty yards' range dropped one of them. The other immediately reined in. He did it so violently that his pony sat back on its haunches. Then he wavered as he turned about—afraid to go on, yet uncertain of what to do next.

An Apache was racing for the west side cliffs. He was an easier target, for he was moving across Catsfoot's line of vision and a single shot from a re-sighted gun stopped him.

The four others had splashed through the water and were moving to Catsfoot's right. And here the situation was critical. They were making directly for the cave where Doc Fulton and Lieutenant Anderson had taken refuge. They had had more time than the others. And, having roughly located where the shots were coming from, they were all stretched flat over the backs of their ponies, offering almost no target.

They were only a few yards from the cave when Catsfoot again used his guns. . . .

There was no possibility of accurate shooting in the split seconds which were left. Somehow, sheer

weight of fire must be used in the hope of preventing
that cave being reached.

Catsfoot had four live shells left in his right hand
Peacemaker, four in the other. He used the pair
together, sending a lead curtain screeching across
the cave mouth and in front of the Apaches. But
those Apaches did not rush into it. At the vital last
moment they recognised their danger and wheeled
off at an angle, seeking fresh cover. In a confused
huddle, they galloped back to the water.

Then they saw him—saw Catsfoot. . . .

They hesitated, pointing and glaring towards the
mouth of the canyon. But only for a few seconds.
Then their minds were made up. The Apaches,
knowing that they had little chance of survival in
that confined space, decided to charge their way
out—to attack directly the man who was bottling
them up.

Catsfoot had expected this. And he had been
confident of holding his position in the narrow space.
But he had not been able to foresee the amount of
rapid fire which had been necessary to protect the
doctor and the lieutenant. He had not thought that
at this critical phase he would be left with two
empty guns.

For now all twelve shells had been expended.

At least fifty seconds were needed to reload a
Peacemaker. Already Catsfoot was busy on his
right gun. He had swung out the cylinder and was
pushing out the empty cases with the ejector rod.
But, as he worked desperately, he knew that he

would not be able even to complete that first phase before the Apaches were on him.

He thought: "This is the finish—there's just nothing I can do. . . ." He stiffened himself against the rock. His fingers transferred to the barrels of his guns, so that he could use them as clubs in a last, useless resistance.

Then the explosion came.

A heavy reverberation from the other end of the canyon. And a slug, partly spent, shattered against the cliff a few feet from Catsfoot. It was so utterly unexpected that Catsfoot gave a start, then began to drop behind the boulder. Then he realised that the shot had not been aimed at him. It had been intended for the Apaches and it had been fired by Luke.

Luke's shooting was dangerously inaccurate. But the attempt had served a purpose. It had had a shock effect on the Apaches, too. Not knowing the strength which opposed them, fearing that they may be surrounded by many gunmen, they pulled viciously on their reins, again bringing their ponies to a halt. Then they raced once more for the caves, this time making for those on Catsfoot's left.

Catsfoot now saw Luke clearly. He was far off and sprawled flat among a pile of small stones as he gripped the Merwin Hulbert. At that moment he fired again. His second shot was more successful. One of the Apaches gave a shriek, then rolled to the ground, wounded in the thigh.

Had the Apaches known the true, trifling strength

which was pitted against them, they would certainly not have lost their nerve. But, as it was, they believed themselves hemmed in from all sides. They galloped back to the water. There they dismounted and tried to follow Luke's example by dropping flat.

Luke, excited and encouraged, fired again. But his enthusiasm was much greater than his skill. The bullet travelled much too high, hit a rock directly in front of the Apaches and ricocheted close to them.

But by now the Apaches had taken enough—more than enough. They tossed aside their carbines. Arms aloft, they slowly got to their feet. Seeing this, Catsfoot shouted towards Luke: "Hold it! No need for any more of your shooting . . . it worries me almost as much as the Apaches!"

By now Luke was also on his feet. He made a wild gesture with his gun.

"We ain't takin' no prisoners!" he shouted.

"We sure are," Catsfoot retorted, reloading his guns as he advanced into the canyon.

"But these Injuns are murderers! I say we oughta put 'em out of the way!"

"And I say they won't be harmed! It's mighty stupid to bawl about them being murderers if you want to act like one yourself."

Luke also was closing in on the Apaches. He gave Catsfoot a baffled glare.

"That's mighty smooth talk," he said, "but I don't understand it and I don't want to! All I know is these Injuns killed plenty of innocent folk for no reason I can think of. They'd have killed the rest of us if it'd suited 'em. I'm goin' to finish the whole durned bunch off . . . !"

He levelled his Merwin Hulbert. The Apaches were no cowards. They did not flinch. Their brown faces were expressionless as they stared at Luke.

Now Catsfoot had halted. Each word came as cold and sharp as ice chippings as he said: "If you squeeze that trigger, Luke, *I'll kill you!*"

At first, Luke did not seem to hear. He continued to take careful aim. Then slowly he lowered the gun a fraction. His red bearded jaw fell slack. He looked at Catsfoot with an expression made up of astonishment, confusion and fury.

"Say that again," he called. "Mebbe . . . mebbe I didn't hear you right . . ."

"You heard fine, Luke."

"Y'mean you'd kill me . . . *me!*"

"Yes—if you try to shoot those prisoners."

"You're plumb crazy! You can't do that! . . . I'm not aimin' to harm you."

"Men who surrender aren't aiming to harm you, either, Luke."

"But these are Apaches!"

"They're human beings too. Now listen to me— there's been a whole lot of killing already in this canyon and I haven't liked any of it. But it was a fight against armed men who had a big advantage in numbers, and it was something that had to be done. But the fighting's over. We'll fix these Apaches so they can't do us any harm for a while—but we won't hurt them. Get it?"

Luke was about to answer, but he was interrupted by a clamour from behind him. It was caused by the other whites. They had emerged from their caves and were staring at the Indian captives—staring with eyes which were wild with hate. Most of the men among them were moving ominously forward. Several of them shouted in support of Luke.

"No need to keep them alive . . . !"

"Put lead into 'em, Luke . . . !"

"Mebbe we'd best string 'em up with a rope . . ."

The men grouped themselves round Luke, urging him to destroy the Apaches. Their voices merged into an animal roar.

Catsfoot knew the reason—and in a way he sympathised. These people had suffered horribly at the hands of the Apaches. And they had seen relatives and friends murdered by them. Now they were reacting to one of the most basic human instincts—the lust for revenge. They were also on the edge of becoming a blood-hungry rabble. Such an atmosphere is infectious and those who had up till now kept quiet were gradually adding their voices to the uproar.

An uneasy grin spread over Luke's face. Then he felt Catsfoot's frigid blue eyes on him. There was merciless challenge in them. The grin faded.

But the whites were now threatening to act on their own. They were pushing past Luke and forming a milling circle round the Apaches, one of whom was wounded. Scrawny, half-starved hands stretched out, grabbing the redskins, pulling them, pushing them. The signs were obvious. A few more seconds and the prisoners would be lynched. And, when it was over and reason had taken the place of fury, none would regret it more than those responsible.

Catsfoot pushed through the heaving mob until he reached the already mauled Indians. Several men had pulled an Apache's hands behind his back, while the big-shouldered mule skinner was gripping his throat, on the point of throttling him. The time for mere words was over. Catsfoot's open palm flashed out. It contacted the mule skinner's cheek with a report like a pistol shot. The result was instantaneous. The mule skinner forgot about the Apache. He stared at Catsfoot in abject astonishment, at the same time rubbing a crimson spot on his round face. And the clamour from the crowd suddenly ceased. The mule skinner's breathing became fast and loud. His words when they came were a series of snarls.

"I'm goin' to pull y'apart for that," he said. "Guns or no guns . . ."

Catsfoot then knew that he had achieved what he wanted—he had diverted attention from the helpless Apaches. And he had done it in the most effective way—for it was an odd fact that whereas many men can take an orthodox punch without losing self-control, a comparatively harmless slap usually goads beyond endurance.

The mule skinner hurled himself at Catsfoot . . .

There was nothing skilful about the attack. It was simply a matter of a lowered head and flailing fists. In the ordinary way it would have been a simple matter to have sidestepped. But, the crowd pressed close around him, Catsfoot had no room to do that. There was nothing for it but to face the rush. He managed to knock aside one of the fists. But the other caught him a glancing blow on the side of the head. It was not a particularly heavy punch, but enough to warn Catsfoot that the matter must be settled immediately—if possible, without harming the man.

The mule skinner tried to step back, to give himself space for another assault. But he found himself unable to do so. Catsfoot's hands were holding his biceps. Holding them against the ribs, so that the forearms were useless.

And at the same time, Catsfoot said: "Okay, I hit you and you hit me. Now's the time to call quits. I figure there may be plenty of fighting to do—but not among ourselves and not here."

There was a murmur of agreement from among the more coolheaded. But the mule skinner was not satisfied.

"I'll tear you . . ." he began.

"Mebbe you will," Catsfoot cut in. "But save it till later. Remember—we've got to organise to get clear of this canyon and we ain't got a lot of time to spare."

The mule skinner was simmering down. He saw

the sense of Catsfoot's warning. So did the others.

"Okay," he said, "I never wanted to fight you—so we can forget it. But what about these Injuns. I still don't see why . . ."

"We'll rope them up and leave them here," Catsfoot said flatly. "I'm not giving the reasons again—I figure I've explained enough already to satisfy folks with ordinary good sense."

There was still a hostile atmosphere against the prisoners. But it had become much less violent.

"You win," the mule skinner said.

A length of hide line was taken from one of the ponies. It was used to lash the Apaches' hands and feet together. Then, on Catsfoot's orders, they were carried to the shelter of a narrow cave. The wounded brave would certainly come to no harm through being left alone for a few hours.

Next, the seven Indian ponies were rounded up in the centre of the canyon. Most were nervous and sweating. But they were fairly fresh and in good condition. They were allowed to drink their fill from the stream and to crop the thin grass.

Then the captured carbines and ammunition were laid in a small pile. And all were in excellent order. Indians usually allowed firearms to deteriorate through neglect. But these showed no signs of fouling in the barrel, and there were no traces of rust in the mechanism. That, as Catsfoot pointed out, suggested they had belonged to soldiers of the column which had been massacred only the day before. The theory was confirmed when Steve recognised the initials of the column sergeant which (against regulations) were carved into the heel of a butt. That brought the memory of his lost comrades back to him and with it came a heavy wave of depression. Perhaps it was because he sensed Steve's misery that Catsfoot said: "No time to brood about what's over, son. Right now, I want you to make a count of the ammunition."

Glad to have something to do, Steve knelt beside the pile of carbines. He began by ejecting the unused shells from the magazines. As most of the Apaches had not had time to use their firearms during the fight in the canyon, the full quota of seven rounds came from almost all of them.

Then Steve checked the spare ammunition, which the Apaches kept in skin bags. This amounted to a total of eighty rounds. In all, there was almost a hundred and thirty shells between the seven Spencers.

"That's better than I'd expected," Catsfoot said when Steve made his report.

Then he looked over the crowd of tense, expectant faces.

"Just so we all get it right, I'm going to go over the escape plan again," he said. "Everything depends on us keeping to that plan. There'll be no room for mistakes. . . ."

Catsfoot paused, glancing through the narrow pass out of the canyon, then at the ponies and the guns.

"Besides Steve, Lieutenant Anderson and myself, there're forty-one of you folks," he went on. "That includes four women and three small children. We want to reach Fort Coulter. But we can't do that in one body because we've only nine horses between the lot of us. And there's a special problem concerning Anderson."

"We can't leave him here!" someone said.

"I don't intend to leave him."

"Then how are you goin' to get him out? He can't walk—he can't even ride."

Catsfoot said: "I'll be handling that later. What concerns me right now is that we're going to use every Indian pony to get the women and kids away. I figure each of the children will be able to ride with a woman, so that means we'll have ponies over for three armed men to go with them as escorts. Those who ride to Fort Coulter will travel in a straight line and just as fast as they can. When they get there, they'll tell the garrison commander just what the others are doing. . . ."

Again Catsfoot paused. Then he added slowly: "The others will be moving a different way. And I'll be trying to make certain that the Apaches don't get on the trail of either group. No need for me to explain again how I aim to do that—anyway, it's my worry. Now I'm going to ask Luke to pick out three of the best shots among you to ride to Fort Coulter with the women and children. . . .'

In the middle of the afternoon, seven Indian ponies filed out of the canyon.

Women were mounted on four of the animals and all save one carried a child in front of her. The rest of the party was made up of three hard-faced men carrying Spencer carbines.

When clear of the canyon, they swung west. Swung into the glow of the falling sun and towards Fort Coulter.

All the time, they rode in a careful single file. They were obeying Catsfoot's orders.

Now, with a quarter of their number gone, the canyon seemed oddly empty. And silent. Catsfoot, with Steve and Luke at each side, strode towards the big cave near the entrance. There, in the gloomy depth of it, Doc Fulton was sitting beside Lieutenant Anderson.

Catsfoot asked: "Is he any better?"

"The bleeding's stopped entirely," Doc Fulton said, "and his breathing is regular. I'd say he's doing well."

"Can we move him?"

"Depends on how he's moved—and how far."

"We could make up a sort of stretcher. And it wouldn't be a long trip—no more than a couple of hours."

"I figure he can stand that, if he's handled carefully."

Catsfoot turned to Luke. "Do you think you can fix the stretcher?"

"We've got a blanket or two, and there's some wood around—yep, we can do it."

The doctor hesitated, then said: "I saw some of your shooting out there, Catsfoot. It was good. But I didn't know exactly what was happening and I still don't know what you plan to do. Remember, I've been in this cave all the time and no one's had time to tell me anything."

Quickly, Catsfoot described how the Apaches had been trapped in the canyon and of the departure of the people for the fort.

"They are all mounted," he continued, "but the Apaches will pick up their trail and overtake them long before they reach Fort Coulter—unless . . ."

Doc Fulton stood up. In the dim light he looked extra weary, extra tense.

"Unless what, Catsfoot?"

"Unless I lay a false scent."

The doctor shook his head. "I don't see how we're going to do that . . . and how are the rest of us going to get away? We've no horses and . . ."

Catsfoot interrupted, saying: "Come where there's more daylight and I'll show you something."

They walked to the mouth of the cave. There Catsfoot picked up a dry twig. With it he drew a rough plan on the sandy ground.

"Up here the Gila River takes a northern loop," he said. "That means its nearest point is around three miles from this canyon. At that same place, there's a cluster of mesquite trees. Got it?"

"I've got it—but I don't understand where it gets us."

With the twig, Catsfoot drew a long, wavy line.

"This is the rest of the river, flowing due west. And here, standing close to the river, is Fort Coulter, around a hundred miles off . . ."

Doc Fulton took off his cracked spectacles and blinked short-sightedly at Catsfoot. "Mebbe I've got it wrong," he said, "but have you some sort of notion that we can use the river to reach the fort?"

"You couldn't have put it better, doc."

"Mebbe I couldn't, but I'm still puzzled. We can't swim a hundred miles and we ain't got any boats."

"Remember the trees," Catsfoot said patiently. "We can't make boats from them, but we can fix a couple of rafts. The river's flowing fast, right now— it can float the rest of you to the fort."

The doctor replaced his spectacles. He looked hopeful, but not convinced.

"It's not difficult to make rafts," he conceded. "But first you've got to bring down the trees, then they have to be trimmed and lashed together. For that, you need tools. We've got nothing."

"We've got what the Apaches brought with them. That includes war axes we can use for felling the mesquites, and hide ropes for holding the logs together."

"Hang it!" the doctor said, slapping a fist into his open palm, "I'd never thought of that. We can all be afloat and well away before to-morrow . . . hey, but there's something else! Something mighty important. How about those who've left on the horses—half of them women and kids? You said you'd lay a false scent to cover them. Well, you won't do it by climbing on to rafts!"

"I'll cover both trails," Catsfoot said. "Or, better still, Steve and I will. He wants to stay with me and I have no mind to stop him. I figure we can wipe out the tracks left by the horses *and* those that you folks will make when you walk towards the river. Then I'll make a new trail. I'll fix it so the Apaches follow Steve and me."

"I don't know how you aim to do that," the doctor said, "Although I don't doubt you can. But what happens to you and the kid? You'll deliberately set the Apaches after you! That's crazy!"

"I figure there's a good chance of keeping ahead of them, then giving them the slip," Catsfoot said. "I've been a trail scout most of my time, and I know how the Apaches work . . ."

Thirty minutes later . . .

Gaunt men walked out of the canyon which had been their prison for six weeks. Four of them shared the weight of an improvised litter on which Lieutenant Anderson lay. All except the litter bearers moved in single file—just as those on horses had done earlier.

With Luke leading, they made for the loop of the Gila River. And the mesquite trees.

Catsfoot and Steve watched the last of them vanish through the narrow pass. Then they looked at each other and smiled. Save for the trussed-up Apaches, deep in a cave, they were alone. Then, without speaking, they walked towards their horses.

The animals were already equipped to obliterate trail markings. Behind each of them was a large, loosely-tied bundle of soft plants and long grass. These were roped to the saddles so that as the horses moved, the foliage would drag behind them.

Catsfoot and Steve paused to fill their water bottles from the stream. Then they swung into the saddles and they, too, rode out of the canyon.

The line of men was still within sight when they emerged from the blood-spattered pass. But they did not follow them. First they took up the trail which those on horseback had used. And now Steve saw why Catsfoot had insisted that those who were riding and those on foot should keep to a single file. By doing so, they made it fairly easy for the dragging foliage to destroy the trail marks. For most of the time Steve could see nothing on the hard, dusty ground. But the spoor was clear enough to Catsfoot, who occasionally turned back to go over again parts which had not been completely masked.

It was after they had covered two miles that Catsfoot reined in. "That's enough," he said. "There's not much chance of the Apaches picking up that trail now—not unless we're very unlucky."

At a trot, they returned to the mouth of the canyon. Dusk was gathering as they set off again, this time covering the trail of the men on foot. This was easier to disguise than that left by the horses, being lighter. When they reached the mesquites in the last light of day, the pioneers had just arrived there. Catsfoot nodded with satisfaction when he noted that they had placed a man with a carbine to guard each side of the cluster of trees. The rest were already at work.

A few of the pioneers were townsfolk from the east, who had been planning to start a new life in the south-western territories. They were generally in weaker physical condition than the others and knew little of the craft of tree felling. But the great majority had drawn on reserves of strength. And they were handling the Apaches' axes with skill. Already four slender trunks were flat to the ground. The branches were being trimmed from them. And the steady thud of the axes could be heard at work on other trees.

Luke, an axe dangling from his hand, came up to them.

"It's goin' well," he said. "I reckon we'll have the rafts ready to float inside a few hours." He paused, then asked anxiously: "Any sign of Indians?"

"None," Catsfoot said, "and I think you'll be all right. There's nothing to bring them to the river now your trail's wiped clean. The same goes for the mounted party. But the Apaches will be around the canyon before long."

"How long?"

"That depends on when they start to get anxious about the seven who don't return—and on how far their lodges are from here. I must say I'd feel a whole lot happier if I knew exactly where their camp is located. But I saw no sign of it when I rode this way from Fort Coulter, so I figure it must be in the other direction—somewhere east."

Doc Fulton pushed through the dense undergrowth towards them.

"I've good news about Anderson," he said. "He's conscious and none the worse for the stretcher trip. D'you want to talk to him?"

Catsfoot nodded, and the doctor took them into the centre of the wood. There Anderson was still flat on his stretcher. Under a stubble of beard, his cheeks were sunken, his nose pinched. About him were the signs of a man who had quivered on the threshold of death. But he turned his eyes as Catsfoot stood over him and gave a weak smile.

"The doctor's told me most of what's been happening," Anderson whispered. "Seems like I've got to thank a lot of people for a whole lot of things."

"Don't worry about that now," Catsfoot told him. "With ordinary luck you'll be safe back in Fort Coulter in a couple of days."

The lieutenant looked at Steve. "I'm told you'll be going with Catsfoot," he said.

"That's the plan, sir. I . . . I wanta stay with him."

Anderson looked doubtful. "I'm not sure I shouldn't order you to return with me," he said. "You're still in the army, you know . . ." He smiled again as he saw Steve's dismayed face. Then he added: "But it looks like you've found a new commanding officer, so mebbe it's best for you to string along with him."

They talked for a few more minutes. Then, with darkness settling, Anderson showed signs of weariness.

"Best let him sleep," Doc Fulton said.

Catsfoot and Steve wished the lieutenant good luck and left him.

Returning to the place where the trees were being felled, they found that the first raft was almost complete. A dozen trunks, each about twenty feet tall, were being lashed together.

Steve said: "They don't look safe to me. Won't those logs come apart when they're afloat?"

Catsfoot shook his head. "They'll get firmer because the water will shrink the skin ropes."

They watched for a short time, then Catsfoot told Luke: "We'll be moving off now. I don't expect the Apaches to start anything till after daybreak, but I want to be in the right place when they do."

"You sure you'll be okay?" Luke asked anxiously. "It's a mighty big risk you're running just to keep them Injuns away from us."

"No man can be certain of anything," Catsfoot said. "But I figure we've a durned good chance of coming out alive."

Luke shook Catsfoot and Steve by the hand. Then all the others temporarily stopped work to offer thanks. As they were about to ride away, Luke said: "We'll be seein' you both at Fort Coulter!"

"Yes, at Fort Coulter," Catsfoot repeated.

Still with the foliage trailing behind, they set their horses back in the direction of the canyon. And when they had ridden only a little way, Catsfoot smiled at Steve and said: "You're looking worried, young soldier! No need for it—we'll make out."

Steve tried to smile in return. But he felt a hot stab of fear in his stomach. A fear which even the presence of this legendary trail scout could not entirely dispel.

They did not re-enter the canyon. They stopped in a slight dip in the ground a half-mile from the canyon, and slept on the sage, covered by their saddle blankets. For Steve, it was a fitful rest. For hours he listened to the call of the coyotes. He shivered once when, far away, he heard the snarl of a cougar as it tore apart its prey.

He dropped into an exhausted sleep shortly before dawn. And he awoke soon afterwards because Catsfoot was shaking his shoulder—shaking it quite violently.

"We've got to start moving fast," Catsfoot said. "No time to take any chuck."

Steve rubbed his eyes. "Why? What's wrong?"

"Plenty wrong. Look around you!"

To the north, billowing columns of smoke were to be seen rising above the horizon. The same to the south. And the two other points of the compass.

"Those are Apaches' signals," Catsfoot said. "They're all round us!"

"But how . . . how has it happened? They can't know about us yet!"

Catsfoot was tightening the girth strap of his horse. He said: "I figured we'd have several hours of daylight before the Apaches found what'd happened in the canyon and got themselves organised. Something's happened that I just didn't expect."

"What can have happened?"

"Someone's told the Apaches we were heading for the canyon."

"But who could have done that?"

Catsfoot put the saddle on Steve's horse. Then he said: "It must have been the Brogans. They didn't hear me say where we were going—but they must have guessed by the direction we were taking. I've got to admit those critters are a lot smarter than I'd thought."

Now they were getting into their saddles. For a few seconds Catsfoot looked carefully around him, studying the far distant smoke signals. Then his whole body became stiff, tense.

"Don't move, son," he whispered to Steve. "Don't even wink an eyelid—our lives depend on it . . ."

CHAPTER FIVE

CRAVEN WOUNDS

STEVE could see no reason for the urgent alarm—not at first. The smoke columns were still rising, but they were far off. On all sides the ground rose slightly. And the west wind, springing hot and free from the great desert of Yuma, stirred the long, purple-topped sage.

Catsfoot was speaking again. Speaking very softly, through lips which did not move.

"We've got close company, Steve. There's a big bunch of Apaches in the sage . . . they must have been creeping up on us while we slept . . . they'll come for us any time now . . . when that happens, don't try to get away . . . just keep still . . ."

Steve did not move his head. But out of the corner of his eyes he could see Catsfoot sitting like a statue in the saddle, both hands holding the leathers.

Then they came . . . gradually, as if seeking to add to the nerve-twisting suspense.

First, one brave rose out of the sage directly in front of them. He had been concealed partly by the foliage and partly because he had been lying behind the crest of the slope. Now he stood arrogantly upright, muscular arms folded across a broad,

copper chest. A doeskin band was round his forehead, in the Apaches' custom. But this band was
wider than those normally worn. And it was vividly
painted. That identified him as a sub-chief. A
nine-inch, slightly curved knife hung in a crude
scabbard from his waist. Across his shoulders was
slung a Spencer carbine.

That Apache remained alone on the top of the
slope for a seeming eternity. Then, in obedience
to some signal, the rest of the braves appeared. It
was as though they had risen out of the depth of the
earth. One moment they were invisible. The next,
they too were standing motionless with their chief.
And they formed a circle round the dip. Daring to
turn his head slightly, Steve estimated that there
must be at least twenty of them.

Now the braves moved. They began walking
slowly towards Catsfoot and Steve. It was like the
gradual tightening of a noose.

Catsfoot whispered: "Whatever you do, don't
lose your nerve! Don't try to run for it, Steve.
That's what they want!"

Steve's throat was dry. He was clutching the
saddle pommel to prevent his hands shaking. But
his brain was clear. He knew the reason for
Catsfoot's warning. The Apaches were hoping to
enjoy one of their death sports—a sport in which
they forced their victims to try to escape from a
circle of braves. Then they would head them off at
every point. But they would not kill immediately.
They would wait until those in the trap were ex-

hausted, helpless with terror. Then, and only then, would they close in for the ghastly kill . . .

The only chance of survival lay in refusing to run. In defying the basic instinct which demanded that one should gallop for any opening between the braves. For if the victims did not move, the Apaches would find little satisfaction in an immediate killing. They would probably wait to find some other means of causing torment before death.

Steve's horse sensed the tension. It was breaking into a thick sweat. It tossed its head, the whites of its eyes showing. Then backed several yards and whinnied.

"Keep him still!" Catsfoot warned. "Take hold of those reins, son!"

Steve realised that, with his hands on the pommel, he had abandoned all control of the animal. Frantically, he transferred his grip to the leathers.

The Apaches were still walking towards them. Most of them had carbines, which they were carrying with the butts tucked under their armpits. Others had cruelly barbed war arrows strung to their bows.

When they were fifty paces away they halted. The chief waved an arm. In obedience to the command, rifles were raised to shoulders, arrows were drawn back against straining gut.

Catsfoot remained motionless. But he said to Steve: "Close your eyes, son—you'll find it easier that way . . ."

But Steve could not do that. Fear compelled him

to watch. To gaze into the black carbine barrels, to stare at the thin arrow heads.

Brown fingers squeezed the triggers of the Spencers and released the arrows . . .

Steve saw the flash as mixtures of saltpetre, sulphur and charcoal exploded in the cartridges. In the same moment he was aware of a ragged crash of sound. And the ground around him became alive. Long streaks appeared in the sage, where bullets cut through it before burrowing deep into the earth, and arrows quivered in the hard soil.

Steve's horse reacted to the noise. Ears flat, it tried to break into a wild gallop. But Steve pulled hard on the leathers. Too hard, for it twisted its head and began running in a small tight circle. Steve heard Catsfoot shout: "Hold it in, son! The Apaches are wanting our horses to break loose!"

But it was a powerful animal and it was in a state of near-hysteria. Unable to gallop in a straight line, it continued circling to the right. Already feeling dizzy, Steve jerked the left rein. In his terror, he again pulled much too violently and the horse began a weird, sideway dance, rearing its front legs, then throwing up its quarters. In that moment Steve knew that the struggle was hopeless. Soon his strength would fail, the horse would rush towards the Indians—and the death sport would begin . . .

Then Catsfoot was at his side.

Catsfoot was leaning from his own saddle and lifting Steve towards him. Lifting him with a single arm wrapped round his waist, and lowering him to the ground. Steve swayed there a few seconds, breathless and still dizzy. He saw his own animal, freed of restraint, rush towards the circle of Indians, turn away, then come to a twitching halt.

Meantime, Catsfoot had taken hold of Steve's wrist. "They're going to try again," he said. "This time the shooting will be closer. Keep your nerve..."

It was much closer. Bullets cut furrows only a few feet from them and several arrows grouped themselves even nearer. Catsfoot muttered: "They don't *want* to finish us yet, so we'll just have to hope they don't have any accidents."

Steve realised that Catsfoot was thinking of the Apaches' notoriously poor marksmanship. In trying to scare them by close shooting, one of them might make a mistake . . .

But there was no third volley. Instead, the ring of braves resumed their walk. They converged in a packed mass. In a vague way, they made Steve think of locusts. The circle grew denser as it drew nearer. Then suddenly the Apaches were pressing round Catsfoot, Steve, and the horse, pressing so hard that it seemed that they would be crushed. The stink of semi-naked bodies was in their nostrils. Vilely-painted faces peered into theirs. Steve was jostled some distance from Catsfoot. The isolation made him yet more afraid till he felt he would be sick because of his sheer concentration of terror. He attempted to call to Catsfoot, but his voice would not carry over the rumbling talk of the Apaches.

But abruptly, there was silence. The chief had

pushed his way through the mass. He was standing opposite Catsfoot. For a time they stared at each other—the dark, massively built Apache and the tall, trail scout whose fair hair fell to his shoulders.

The Apache said in slow English: "You have courage and that is good. Men of courage can be made to die slowly."

Catsfoot did not answer. But his eyes remained fixed on the Apache.

"Have you no tongue that you do not speak?" the Apache asked.

This time Catsfoot gave a taut smile. He said: "This doesn't seem like the time for talking except for one thing . . ." He hesitated.

"Tell me, for I listen."

"The boy . . . I guess you're going to kill me, but I want you to let him go unharmed."

The Apache turned and the crush of braves parted so that he could look at Steve.

"Among our people, boys such as he are already riding with the warriors."

"But he's only a kid and . . ."

"He wears the clothing of a soldier. And does he not ride with those who would take our lands and food from our people? Let him then die as a soldier." He turned again to Catsfoot and asked: "How do they speak of you?"

"Folks call me Catsfoot. I'm a trail scout."

"I had thought it, for I have heard much of you. This is a capture indeed for me, Earo, first son of Cochise."

At the sound of the last name, Catsfoot showed a faint hint of surprise.

"You are Cochise's eldest son?"

"It is even so. My father is the greatest of all warriors. Greater even than I."

Catsfoot nodded. "I have met your father," he said quietly. "He speaks well of me."

Earo's right hand whipped out. His powerful fingers grabbed Catsfoot's loose buckskin jacket at the chest. He pulled, trying to draw Catsfoot still closer to him. But Catsfoot had braced himself and spaced his legs for the strain. He did not move. Slowly, Earo released his grip and let his hand drop. But his face was working with fury.

"You lie, as all whites lie! Had you spoken to my father Cochise, you would not be alive to-day! Is he not the chief of all the Apaches? Is he not the enemy of all your people?"

"He's the enemy of our people," Catsfoot said, "but I do not lie when I tell you I have spoken with him. It happened nearly a year ago, not far from a town called Gloryrise. He spared my life because he kept his word—and I kept mine."*

The fury faded from Earo's face. It became thoughtful. "My father did speak of some such pledge," he said. "But such things do not matter now. Were he here, he would slay you—even as I shall slay!"

Catsfoot knew that this was true. Having given their word, the Apaches usually—although not

* Told in "Gun Town Marshal," by John Robb.

always—kept it. But sentiment or mercy was not part of their make-up. They had scant regard for their own safety and no respect whatever for the sanctity of white lives. With the Cheyenne and Kiowa nations, most of them regarded war as the highest human activity. Before the coming of the whites, the Apaches had terrorised smaller and peaceful tribes in Arizona and New Mexico. Now they faced by far their greatest challenge—and they also had some justice on their side . . .

Hunters, with their extremely accurate ·50 Sharps rifle, were slaughtering the buffalo herds upon which the Apaches lived. The whites killed the bison only for their hides, for which they received a maximum of five dollars each in the great market at Dodge City. But the Apaches used every part of the animal—the skins for clothing, teepees, beds, and (stretched across frames) to make bull boats for river crossings. They also were treated to make saddles, halters, belts and hair ornaments.

Neither was any part of the flesh wasted. The finest meat came from the hump-ribs, but even the intestines were consumed. And the dried dung made good fires.

Now, with the building of the Santa Fé, Union Pacific and other railroads over the plains, the buffalo slaughter was rapidly increasing. And with it came a threat of starvation for the Apaches. They would gladly have fought the white settlers for no other reason than sheer love of battle. But they fought now with extra fanatical fury, knowing that their survival was at stake. Attempts had been made by the government in Washington, acting through Indian agencies, to enter into pacts with the Apaches, guaranteeing them reservations and regular food supplies. But such treaties, even when solemnly signed, seldom lasted long. On the one hand, it was almost impossible for the government to prevent whites entering the reservations in defiance of the pacts. On the other, the Apaches only entered into treaties to give themselves time to recover from battle losses. They were quick to seize upon any reason—however trivial—for declaring a treaty void.

Such facts were at the back of Catsfoot's mind when he realised that there was little hope for either Steve or himself at the hands of Earo and his braves.

He heard Earo repeating: "My father, Cochise, would slay you, even as I shall slay . . ."

Catsfoot said "And slay slowly, I guess."

"Until your courage breaks. Until you weep for mercy and tell me where my white captives from the canyon have fled, for . . ."

He broke off and turned round. Two men on Indian ponies had mounted the crest of the rise. For a moment they paused there, before cantering towards them. They were big men, and they were grinning with humourless, wanton delight.

They were two of the Brogan brothers.

Earo showed no emotion as the Brogans dismounted and pushed through the cluster of braves towards him. But he stepped aside so that the two men were face to face with Catsfoot. They were still grinning. One of them said: "You ain't been so smart, Catsfoot. We figured there was no other place you could go to but the canyon, when you had the wounded officer with you. And we had a nice slice of luck—we made contact with Earo early last night and he put a watch on the canyon. It seems like you got them prisoners away, but that don't matter none. You'll soon be persuaded into tellin' us where they are."

Catsfoot ignored the threat. Instead, he glanced at the Brogans' gun belts.

"Seems the Apaches have fixed you up well," he said. "You've got guns again."

"Sure we've got guns. Earo looks after his friends—don't you, Earo?"

There was a flicker of contempt in Earo's expression as he stared at the Brogans. He did not answer.

The brother who was doing the talking stared towards Catsfoot's waist. "Talkin' about guns, I see they haven't lifted yours from you yet. Looks like you hadn't the nerve to use 'em."

Catsfoot said softly: "Like to test me? Just feel for your gun . . . and you'll have an answer."

"We ain't had an even draw against you, Catsfoot. I figure either me or m'brother could fix you."

"That suits me . . . just go ahead and draw— both of you!"

The Brogans stepped back a pace, to give themselves extra space. Both of them lowered their right hands until the tips of their fingers were quivering over their gun butts. Catsfoot's voice was taunting as he said: "Pull your guns! This'll be an even draw—two of you against one!"

The Brogans took a swift glance at each other. Then they, too, dropped their hands.

"No need for us to put lead into you, Catsfoot. I figure the Apaches are goin' to fix you. I sure look forward to seein' you yell for mercy. There's a . . ."

Earo moved forward. "Enough has been spoken," he said. Then he gestured to his braves and added a few words in the Apaches' patois. Catsfoot was seized from behind by several braves. He struggled against the overwhelming force and managed to drag one arm free. Then a leg was twisted between his ankles, he lost balance and fell.

The Apaches dropped on him like hounds on meat. They drove long wooden stakes into the ground with their axes. They held Catsfoot flat on his back while they lashed his wrists and legs to those stakes. And when they rose he was spread-eagled, unable to stir more than his head.

Again the Brogans elbowed to the front. They glowered over Catsfoot. Their eyes were crazed with triumph. One of them shouted at him: "You won't be slingin' your guns no more!"

The other said: "It'd be a nice idea if we cut you down to size ourselves—right now . . ."

They exchanged glances. And they understood each other. Their guns came out.

They drew them in the unhurried manner of men who had time to spare and were determined to squeeze the last drop of pleasure from the fact.

Steve heard a couple of clicks as they flipped back the hammers. He also heard a Brogan say: "How about a slug in your hands, Catsfoot . . . ? just for a start before the Injuns get to work on you . . ." He saw Catsfoot's hands instinctively contract under the threat of the bullets which, at such short range, would smash every bone in them.

Several Apaches were standing between Steve and the Brogans. All were heavy men. But Steve had the strength which comes of frenzy. Head down, he butted through them. He was vaguely aware of a jarring pain in the neck as the top of his skull crashed against a thighbone. The hilt of an Apache's sheathed knife scratched his cheek. Then he was at the Brogans . . .

He threw himself on them like a shot from a gun, feet kicking, fists whirling. His knuckles slammed an iron-hard chin. He had a blurred impression of the two men staggering against each other. At the same moment there was a double crash from the Brogans' guns. In that open space there was no echo. As the crisp report died away, a new sound was to be heard. It was a long, low groan. It came from Catsfoot.

Catsfoot was convulsing against the ropes which held him down. His face was twisted.

Blood was welling from his right hand and his left arm.

CHAPTER SIX

A PLACE TO HIDE

STEVE was kneeling beside Catsfoot—the Brogans forgotten, the Apaches forgotten . . .

Catsfoot was breathing quickly and noisily, as men do when in a struggle against acute pain. His back was arched, his lips drawn back against his teeth, his eyes were glazed and heavy.

Automatically, Steve remembered his army medical training. He looked at the right hand. A slug had cut a shallow furrow across the muscle under the thumb. That was the limit of the damage. But the left arm was a different matter. There, a bullet had sliced through the buckskin sleeve just below the elbow. The white of the bone was visible. Obviously the bone had been grazed near the nerve junction. But in neither case had the bullet lodged in the flesh.

Steve removed his neckerchief, tore it in halves and roughly bandaged the wounds. As he did so Catsfoot's breathing became easier and his body relaxed. He was getting over the first agonising shock.

"You'll be okay," Steve whispered to him. "These'll heal."

But as he uttered the words he realised their futility. Those wounds would never be given the chance to heal. Catsfoot was doomed—both of them were doomed—at the hands of the Apaches.

Earo was standing over them. Suddenly aware of the fact, Steve twisted and looked up. And he shouted frantically: "He can't fight any more! Why don't you cut the ropes? Or are you still scared of him—even with two useless hands?"

For a few moments Earo's lean face was expressionless. Then he muttered an order. Two braves slashed the skin lines which held Catsfoot down. Steve took off his tunic, folded it, put it under Catsfoot's head.

"Thanks, son," Catsfoot panted. "I wish I could be doing something to help you . . . I guess this is a bad way for both of us to go out—just not being able to put up a fight . . ."

But Steve was hardly listening. His eyes and his mind were held by two objects—Catsfoot's guns. No one had bothered to take them from him. They had always been useless, anyway, against such odds. Now they remained in their holsters—long-barrelled, glistening new and lethally efficient ·45 Peacemakers. Catsfoot could not even grip their curved butts. But they were within easy reach of Steve. Just a few inches away. A quick snatch and he could have them out. With them he might be able at least to finish the Brogans. Then they would be going down fighting. Catsfoot could no longer use his guns. But Catsfoot's guns could still be *used*. Maybe they could crash just once more. Once more in the cause of justice . . .

Both guns? No, that would be more than he could manage. Better just to go for one of them—the one in the left holster, which was the nearer.

Steve shifted his position slightly, so that he could more easily swing round on his knees to aim at the Brogans. He braced himself for the snatch at the holster . . .

Then Earo spoke. His deep voice had a numbing effect.

"Boy, do not try anything foolish," he said.

Again Steve looked up at the chief, bewildered that he should have guessed. But when Earo spoke again there was a new, a strange undertone to his words. They were not addressed to Steve. They were spoken directly to Catsfoot.

"We are men, you and I," he was saying. "You seek to slay me or I wish to slay you—but we do not spit on each other. That is the law between warriors, even between the Apaches and the white men. It was my wish to break your courage before I killed you. But that is no longer possible, for I would only be finishing the work which other whites have begun." Then he looked at the Brogans. They had changed, those Brogans. Their confidence, their fiendish delight, were gone. They shuffled uneasily. Earo went on: "These brothers have injured my captive. That is the same as stealing my food. So I, Earo, will give justice to all of you . . ."

He paused, staring again at Catsfoot. "You and the boy," he said, "may leave this place. We shall not harm you until ten days and ten nights have passed. That is my word. And these, the brothers," he looked at the Brogans, "they will stay here until the sun sinks. Then they also will be allowed to leave unharmed and it will be thus for ten days and ten nights. The brothers will have that time to find you and kill you, Catsfoot. And you, with hands which can no longer shoot, will have the same time to find a way to kill the brothers. Where any of you go I care not, save that you will not be allowed to reach the fort or the towns, for my braves will always be watching you."

There was a long incredulous silence. Then, in a voice weak with pain, Catsfoot asked: "What happens if all of us are still alive at the end of the ten days?"

"Then my braves will slay all of you, for all will have failed."

"And if one of us kills the other?"

"He who is victorious will not be harmed and may then go to the fort or anywhere else. I set white men to destroy white men, with a sure death the price of failure. That is my justice . . ."

Steve stood up shaking with fury.

"What chance will Catsfoot have? His gun hands are useless and they'll be that way for a long time."

"I am wondering," Earo said. "It will be good to find out, for I know he will not easily give up his life—or yours."

They had been riding for three hours, always

heading south. Their horses had never exceeded a
steady walk, for Catsfoot could scarcely control his
mount. The reins were looped over his bandaged
right hand. When he kept it still, he was aware only
of a dull throbbing. But the slightest attempt to use
it made the finger muscles lock solid, the entire hand
becoming a slab of concentrated pain. His left arm
was now in a sling which Steve had fixed. From
elbow to wrist, it felt as if raw flame were scorching
the flesh from within.

During the hours since they had left the Apaches,
Steve had constantly watched Catsfoot. Several
times he was tempted to ask him if he wished to
rest, or whether he wanted the dressings adjusted.
But he did not do so because he sensed that Catsfoot
wanted silence—silence to adjust himself to un-
ceasing pain, and to think.

When the time came for talk, Catsfoot would
begin it . . .

And that time arrived when Catsfoot suddenly
gave Steve a brief, tense smile and said: "Don't
look so worried, son! We're still alive and with any
luck we'll stay that way."

At first, Steve did not reply. He instinctively
turned in the saddle and glanced back.

"What's wrong?" Catsfoot asked.

"I've just been wondering . . ." Steve began.

"What about?"

"About the Brogans. They start after us at sun-
set—that's around six hours from now. D'you think
we'll be able to keep far enough ahead of them?"

Steve was surprised to see Catsfoot shake his head.

"We haven't a chance if we just try to keep in front," he said. "They might pick up our trail and overhaul us. Or else we'd fold with exhaustion."

"But what else can we do?" Steve asked. "If they catch us now, we're done! You can't use your guns and I wouldn't have any kind of chance against the Brogans."

"We've got to find a place where I can rest up for a few days. Give me a week at the most and I figure I'll be able to use these hands of mine. Then I can go after the Brogans, instead of them coming after me. Remember, son, I've got to get them before ten days are out."

Steve doubted very much whether Catsfoot's hands would be anything like usable in that time. But he let the point pass. Instead he asked: "Where *can* we find a place to rest? We can't go to the canyon, because they're sure to look for us there. We can't try to reach Fort Coulter or any of the towns, because the Apaches won't let us. All that's left is open territory."

Catsfoot said: "There's Karlsbergh."

Steve looked sharply up at him.

"Karlsbergh? That sounds like a town! We can't . . ."

"It's the name of a town all right," Catsfoot said, "and we ought to be there inside of two hours."

Steve scratched his head, doubly puzzled.

"I've never heard of the place. Never knew

there was any white settlement nearer than Fort Coulter."

"There isn't."

Steve stared at Catsfoot's pain-lined face, which was smiling again.

"I give up," he said. "Mebbe you'll explain."

"Gladly, Steve. Karlsbergh's a ghost town."

"Y'mean a place where no one lives any more?"

"That's right. It sprang up around twenty years ago, when copper deposits were found nearby. For a while it boomed and mebbe four or five hundred folks lived there. But before the Civil War started, the copper started to run out and the people began leaving the town, too. Then, when the war got going and the soldiers were pulled out of this territory, the whole remaining population fled for Tucson and Phoenix, or east for the safety of Santa Fé. Quite a few of them never got any place, because the Apaches cut them off and massacred them. Since then, Karlsbergh's just been a main street and a few empty buildings."

"Doesn't *anyone* go there at all?"

"Not often. There's nothing to go there for. Everything worth looting was taken by the Apaches long ago. But there's shelter there and it's a place most people have forgotten about—if they have ever heard of it. That's why I'm thinking there's an even chance that the Brogans won't think of heading that way. They'll figure on us trying to get as far from them as we can. So even if they do know about

Karlsbergh, they may think it unlikely we'll be there. Anyway, that's how I'm hoping things'll work out, because right now I can't think of anything else we can do."

As he considered it, Steve was uneasy. The Brogans knew the territory well, so it seemed very possible that they had at least heard of the ghost town. And that they were cunning had been shown by the way they directed the Apaches to the canyon. Yet, as Catsfoot had said, to try merely to keep ahead of them would be fatal. Catsfoot was in no condition to endure days in the saddle. And being able only to move slowly, they would probably be overtaken by the Brogans.

Yes, although there was danger in Karlsbergh, it was the only chance.

Steve recalled hearing that, scattered over the vastness of the territory, there were several such ghost towns. Some had sprung up as the railroads were being built. For a time, these had prospered on the free-spending gangers who were laying the tracks, and on the pay of the soldiers who guarded them. Then, as the railroads moved on, the people left, too. Other towns, like Karlsbergh, were the result of copper or gold strikes. They appeared practically overnight, and became deserted as quickly.

There were other places in Arizona of which not even the empty buildings remained. These were towns which the Apaches had attacked during the Civil War and burned to the ground. Places where men, women and children fought to the death in a hopeless defence of their lives and homes. They were not truly ghost towns, for they no longer existed, save perhaps for charred scatterings of wood which marked where framewood buildings had stood.

Suddenly Catsfoot broke into Steve's thoughts. He was saying: "You learned a bit about doctoring with the cavalry, eh?"

"It was part of my job. Bugle boys have to learn to look after the wounded till a doctor can get to them."

Catsfoot hesitated. Then he asked: "My hands . . . how bad are they?"

"Your right hand isn't so seriously hurt. The thumb muscle's torn, but it ought to mend without trouble."

"And the left . . . ?"

"That's not so good. It ought to get better, too, if it's kept clean—but it'll take time."

"How much time?" Catsfoot rapped out the question.

"I don't know enough about it to tell you for certain. But I'd say at least a couple of weeks before it can come out of the sling."

Catsfoot gave an impatient grunt. "It's got to be a lot less than that, son. If I don't get the Brogans inside ten days, we're all dead meat."

Then they were silent again. The only sound was the slow rhythm of hoofs. But a single, stark thought was revolving round Steve's mind. "He'll never be able to use his guns in ten days," he kept telling himself. "We're finished . . ."

The ghost town of Karlsbergh lay before them. Just a single street . . .

Alkali dust eddied and swirled over the pitted track. A broken wagon wheel lay in the centre of it. On each side were the framewood buildings, the doors were torn off all of them. On some, the roofs had collapsed. Others sagged at grotesque angles where support beams had rotted. Every window frame was smashed. Outside those buildings, most of the planking had dropped from the board-walks.

Everywhere, cacti and sagebrush were growing. They sprouted in patches on the street, on the walls, even out of what had been the water pump at the north end of the town.

Once people had lived here. Copper miners had argued their metal weights in an assay office. Women had gossiped outside a busy general store. Cold-eyed buffalo hunters had ridden in to spend hours in a brawling saloon. A town marshal had enforced the federal law from a combined office and lock up. Many had worshipped in a tiny chapel . . .

It had been a place of the worst and the best, of happiness and misery, of generosity and greed. It had been alive. Now it was dead, decaying, hushed. Steve looked at it with revulsion.

"I never thought any place could look like this," he said. "It's like a bad dream."

Catsfoot nodded. "It's not pleasant. But we'll get used to it—we've got to. Come on . . ."

They rode past the remains of the town stables and into the street. The hoof beats echoed weirdly amid the loneliness of the place.

Catsfoot reined in opposite a small one-storey building. This was in slightly better condition than most others. The walls were still erect and there was only one small hole in the roof. A battered sign outside revealed that it had been the assay office and faded lettering announced: *Matthew Wilcox, Federal Metals Inspector*. Steve wondered whether Wilcox was still alive, or had he fallen to the Apaches during the flight for safety?

They dismounted and secured their horses to a single post which had once been part of a hitching rail.

"Be careful on the boardwalk," Catsfoot warned. "There's not much planking left, and what there is will be rotted."

They trod cautiously into the building. Steve stopped when just within the threshold. He had to fight a temptation to turn and run from the place. The counter where the metals had been weighed was still there and little damaged. But the protective steel grille which had been fixed along its length was partly ripped away. A pair of scales lay on the floor and several fine weights were scattered about. A wood-burning stove lay on its side. Beside it was a scattering of glass in a smashed picture frame. The picture was recognisable—it was a lithograph

depicting Abraham Lincoln at the time of his first
election to Congress in 1846.

Behind the counter, an open doorway led into
what had been the assay officer Wilcox's living
room.

Dust lay everywhere, grey alkali dust, spreading
like a shroud.

Steve muttered: "Mebbe we'll get used to this
place, but right now I'm liking it less and less."

"Keep quiet, son!" Catsfoot murmured.

Surprised, Steve looked up at him. That steely
look was back in Catsfoot's eyes. He was staring at
the floor. Then Steve saw it, too. The dust on the
floorboards had been disturbed. There was a
distinct furrow which led through a gap at the far
end of the counter, through the office and into the
living room. No animal could have made those
tracks. The width and length could only have been
created by human feet.

Catsfoot leaned down so that he could whisper in
Steve's ear.

"Don't get scared," he said, "whoever it is,
mebbe he's gone. Or if he's still here, he could be
friendly. But there's no sense in taking chances.
Take one of my guns . . ."

Steve lifted Catsfoot's left gun from its holster.

"Follow me," Catsfoot added. "Keep the Colt
out of sight unless things look awkward."

Now Steve knew beyond doubt why Catsfoot had
been given his name. Despite the fact that his hands
were useless, depriving him of some balance, he

moved in complete silence. Yet he moved swiftly, too, somehow avoiding those boards which would have creaked under his weight. Steve tried to duplicate his steps in the hope of also moving without sound. But he knew that his boots were making some noise, although it was slight.

They followed the disturbed dust to the inner door. And there Catsfoot halted. It took Steve a couple of seconds to come up behind him. Then, peering past Catsfoot's shoulder, he looked into the room.

He saw an untidy pile of blankets under the opposite wall. Close to them was a small, unpainted table. Four throwing knives lay on that table, arranged neatly side by side. And within reach of them stood a man—a vicious, dwarf of a half-breed.

He was little more than five feet tall. His face was like a dried nut, shrivelled brown. High cheekbones strained against the skin. The mouth was a shapeless slit, pulled back against his teeth in a snarl. Small eyes showed as dark pits, with the shades of madness in them. Yet power was in his small body, as it crouched forward like an animal about to spring. Power was there in the width of the shoulders under a tattered Indian doeskin jacket, in the thick wrists, and in the sinewy fingers which held the gleaming blade of another throwing knife. He was holding it delicately, yet confidently.

His mouth scarcely moved as he said: "You have come for Gallota? Come and take me . . . !"

Each word spoken was a separate blast of hatred.

"We haven't come for you or anyone else," Catsfoot said evenly. "We're just looking for shelter for a few days."

"I don't believe . . . Gallota believes no one! You want to kill me!"

Catsfoot glanced down at his hands. "I can't do much harm to anyone right now. It's like I said, we've just . . ."

"So if you don't want me, there's nothing for you here! Go! Go before I kill!"

"We're not going to harm you and we're not leaving here, either," Catsfoot said.

At that moment, Steve moved slightly, so that he stood to one side of Catsfoot, instead of behind him. Too late, Steve realised that he had made a mistake. The gun he was holding showed clearly. And the ebony eyes of Gallota had seen it. The half-breed's lips stretched further back. From somewhere in the depth of his throat came a snarl.

"So . . . ! You get a kid to do the killing for you! Mebbe that is good. Now you will see how I use my blades. . . ."

His arm did not move much. But his wrist gave a quick flick. There was a blur as the blade sped across the room. Steve felt a sudden backward pull at his right arm. Under the shock of it, the gun clattered to the floor. Numbed with confusion and fright, he stared at his sleeve. The knife had sliced through the material. Yet his skin was not even marked.

The half-breed laughed. It was a shrill, hysterical sound, almost like the cry of an animal.

"Now you know, uh? You both see how I can protect myself!"

"All right," Catsfoot said, "so we know you can toss a knife. Now let's see if we can have a sensible talk."

Gallota had plucked another knife from the table. He caressed it. "No talking! The kid came to kill me so mebbe I'll fix both of you!"

"I tell you he was only . . ."

But again Gallota interrupted. He shouted at Steve: "Your gun's at your feet. Pick it up!"

Steve had no choice. To show that he had no intention of trying to use it, he gripped it by the barrel. But Gallota did not want that.

"Put your hand round the butt, kid . . . good! Now a finger on the trigger . . . !"

Trying not to show his fear, Steve obeyed. But he held the gun loosely at his side.

"Aim at me," Gallota ordered.

"But I . . ."

"Aim the gun at me! Aim it at my heart! Do it . . . !" His voice broke off in a wild scream.

Steve looked desperately at Catsfoot and their eyes met. That the half-breed was crazed was obvious. So was the fact that he intended to murder both of them.

"I am giving you a chance," Gallota was screaming again. "I am fair! I am generous! I will not throw my knife till you have taken aim at me and we will see . . . we will see if I can throw a blade faster than you can squeeze a trigger! Go on . . . aim and shoot . . . !"

Gallota was fantastically fast with a knife, as were many half-breeds. But even so, his challenge would have been suicidal, save for one fact—the Peacemaker which Steve held was not cocked. A flip of the thumb would bring the hammer back. But that would grant a vital second to Gallota. Squeezing the trigger would have the same effect, it being a double-action weapon. But again, there would be a moment when the rise of the hammer would be visible to the half-breed. The recent demonstration showed that a mere flash of time was all that the knife expert needed. He knew exactly what he was doing when he challenged Steve.

"Aim and shoot, I said . . . !" He was screaming again. The glint of insanity was in his dark eyes. His tiny face was twitching. Catsfoot breathed: "Don't do it, Steve! He needs an excuse to kill you . . . keep your arm down whatever happens!"

The dwarf half-breed had overheard. Abruptly, his tones became soft as he said to Catsfoot: "Excuse? I need no excuse! The kid will have a count of three to put up his gun and try to shoot . . . if he hasn't done so by then, I will throw this knife and this time I will do more than cut his sleeve!"

Catsfoot gave a hopeless glance at his bandaged right hand and at his left arm in the sling. Then he said: "Why don't you wait a few days? Mebbe it won't be so long before *I* can use my guns—then if you still feel like this kind of sport, you can try me."

Gallota looked at Catsfoot's holsters, one with a Peacemaker in it, the other empty. He said, "You sling two guns. Why?"

"Because that's the way I like it—two's company."

"I want a real answer, mister! Most men get along all right with just one gun. Why do you pack a couple? Do you figure it'll make folks twice as scared of you?"

Now there was a taunt in his voice. But Catsfoot was carefully calm. "Sometimes a man can have a bad cartridge in his gun," he said. "If that happens when you need to shoot in a hurry, you're not likely to live so long. The double-draw's a precaution."

"Yeah, that's the right answer," Gallota said, looking faintly interested. "But not many men can draw two guns at the same time—not draw them fast."

"I guess that's so, but I manage."

"You talk like you're a real fast gun."

When Catsfoot spoke again, Steve knew that he was deliberately diverting the half-breed's mind.

"I figure I'm the fastest gun in the new territories," he said.

"That's big talk when you don't have to prove anything!"

"I can't prove it right now—but why don't you wait till my hands are right?"

Gallota was half-impressed. He said: "I can toss a knife faster than any man can pull a gun."

"Any man except me," replied Catsfoot quietly.

"You bluff good—what's your name?"

"Catsfoot."

Gallota tensed. Then he said: "You could be lying. I know about this hombre Catsfoot, but I don't know it's you."

"Wait a little time and be sure," Catsfoot said softly.

"Mebbe I will. I've always known I could kill even Catsfoot with my blades. If you *are* Catsfoot, I could do m'self a good turn. But before I make up my mind, I'd like to know just why you are in this ghost burgh."

"A couple of gun-slingers are after us—name of Brogans."

A pink and tiny tongue slipped out and licked dry lips. "This gets kinda interestin' to me. I heard of the Brogans, too. They're fast guns—real fast. But there was always three of 'em."

"There still is three of them, but one is taking a rest."

"That so? Why?"

"I put a slug into him."

"You beat one of the Brogans to the draw! If that's true, you must be Catsfoot. Okay . . . take off the bandages and feel for your guns!"

Catsfoot shrugged. "I can't take them off yet. My hands are badly hurt. I need time."

Gallota's voice returned to a shrieking bellow. "You've had all the time you'll get! I've fixed a lot of hombres with my knives—that's why I have to hide out here for a while. Now I aim to fix you . . . it'll sound good when word gets around that I finished Catsfoot . . . that'll make me real important! Folks won't laugh behind my back because I'm small . . . not when they know I killed you . . . no, I ain't lettin' this chance slip . . ."

His wrist flicked again. This time, the knife travelled even faster than before. As it spun, it sliced off part of the brim of Catsfoot's fedora. And it ended, quivering, in the wall behind his head. At the same moment, Gallota took up another knife. He tested the point with the tip of a finger.

When he looked up, his face was working with frenzy. And he asked: "You will not take off your bandages?"

"I can't, and it'd be no use if I could. Like I told you, my hands are no good."

For the barest moment, Gallota hesitated. And a strange, utterly new expression flickered over his face, almost softening it. It was as though a part of the half-breed which had seldom had a chance to influence him, had suddenly asserted itself, the better part, which existed in nearly all men. But the expression vanished in the second that it appeared. Perhaps only Catsfoot saw it and understood it.

"I'll still throw my knife," he said, snarling again. "This time I will not miss. . . !"

CHAPTER SEVEN

DUEL IN DARKNESS

Steve knew that there was no time for him to bring the gun up, to aim and fire it at the half-breed. Only a quivering fraction of time remained before the blade would flash towards a helpless Catsfoot. There was only one chance—he recognised it and took it. With the Peacemaker still hanging loosely in his hand, he jerked at the trigger.

In that confined space, the crash seemed to rock the walls. He felt a wrench on his wrist from the gun's vicious recoil, felt a scorch of flame on his hand from the gas vent. He sensed that a hole the size of a dollar piece had been torn in the boards near his feet.

The explosion came as the knife was leaving Gallota's fingers. Had it come a tenth of a second later it would have been too late. But as it was, the noise caused a reflex action in the half-breed's hand. The knife sped true at a point slightly to the left of Catsfoot's chest. But its spin was misjudged. The razor sharp steel did not slash into the flesh. Instead, the heavy bone haft hit him. It hit Catsfoot so hard that he staggered slightly back.

Gallota screamed something which was beyond understanding. But at the same time he was acting.

Realising that Steve with the gun was a danger, his hand flashed out to grip another blade. But by now, Steve was aiming the Peacemaker at Gallota's head. He was again pulling on the trigger.

But he did not complete the pull. Instead, he jerked the gun aside . . .

For Catsfoot, Gallota and the table were tangled together in ferocious chaos.

Despite his useless hands, Catsfoot had thrown himself across the room. But he had not thrown himself directly at Gallota. Deliberately, he had crashed against the table where two remaining knives were placed. He was in mid-air when one of his shoulders slammed against the edge of it. The flimsy piece of furniture overturned towards Gallota at the moment when the half-breed was lifting the knife from it. The flat of the table, with Catsfoot's weight behind it, collided with Gallota's chest. Gallota, losing balance, forgot the knife. He swept both arms round Catsfoot's neck. And Catsfoot, now falling across the edge of the table, brought Gallota to the floor. The two men hit it with a tremendous crash, Catsfoot squarely on top of Gallota.

There was an instant when they seemed motionless. Then came a new sound—of tearing and splintering. And the decaying floorboards broke under the impact . . .

Between the floor and the bare earth beneath there was a clear eighteen inches. Catsfoot and Gallota dropped into it.

They fell into dusty, murky, semi-darkness. The

only light came from the newly created gap above them. As Gallota instinctively flung out his arms to save himself from injury, the two disentangled. Catsfoot, who had been unable to break his fall, felt momentarily sick with pain. The air had rushed out of his lungs. Bruises on his ribs added to the hurt he had received when the knife haft had hit his chest. But somehow he had kept his injured arm and hand out of danger. Carefully he rolled from his side on to his back. Then he tried to locate Gallota.

The half-breed was a couple of yards away, sprawled on his stomach against one of the joists. That much could be made out in the confined gloom, but no more. Catsfoot could hear him breathing quickly and at the same time mumbling like a man in a feverish sleep. Probably he was dazed.

Slowly, Catsfoot edged towards the hole, pushing himself along with his feet. He saw Steve's face appear and a hand stretched down to help him up.

"Take it easy," Steve said. "You'll soon be out of there. How are your hands?"

"This hasn't done them any good, but I guess it hasn't harmed them any, either," Catsfoot told him, pushing again.

His head was now almost directly under the jagged opening. But he had to take a rest because of a new pain developing in his shoulders. This was caused by loose stones on the hard, sour soil upon which the building had been erected. Being unable to raise himself with his hands, and not having the space even to kneel, the rough surface scratched through his buckskin jacket and jarred against his bones.

Steve, flat on the floor and peering into the half-light, asked anxiously: "Shall I try to lift you through?"

"No need, son. Anyway, not yet. I just need a rest. You can put your hands under my shoulders when . . ."

Catsfoot's voice tailed away. He felt a grip on his ankles, an iron grip which compressed the stiff leather of his saddle boots. Then came a powerful, relentless pull on his legs.

Catsfoot gave a grunt of pain as his back and shoulders again scraped the stones.

He was being dragged away from the opening, being dragged by Gallota far under the floorboards, dragged to a place where every advantage would be with the dwarf, who could move more easily in the tiny space, and who had the use of his hands . . .

Too late, Steve knew what was happening; he tried to grab some part of Catsfoot's buckskins. But already he was out of reach.

Abruptly, the dragging ceased. The grip on the ankles relaxed. Catsfoot heard a shuffling, a cough. Then something touched the centre of his stomach and moved lightly along it. He knew it was Gallota's fingers. Here, they were in all but total darkness. And Gallota was relying on his sense of touch to establish Catsfoot's exact position.

The fingers moved further up—slowly, carefully. They touched his throat and there they paused. But not for long. Suddenly both hands were there. Both sets of fingers were round his neck. And the tiny, but strong thumbs were squeezing his throat, blocking the air to his lungs.

When taken by surprise, a man ceases to think clearly within ten seconds of receiving a strangle-hold. In twenty-five seconds he is unconscious. If the grip remains, death follows in two minutes at the most. Catsfoot knew that. And knew that he must do something—anything—immediately if he were to survive.

His legs were his only weapon. But with the floor boards close above, they could not be raised far, or swung round for a kick at the half-breed. But there was a joist close to his ankles. The joist against which Gallota had lain. Catsfoot saw it vaguely. That might give leverage . . .

But already there was a streak of white agony in his lungs. The fibres of his brain felt as if they were being ground down with sandpaper. There was a temptation not to fight, not to resist. An almost overwhelming desire to lose consciousness as soon as possible, just to get that agony over. But he got the soles of his boots against the joist. With all that remained of his strength, he pushed. At the same time he arched his back. There was a double result. He slid several painful inches across the ground. And Gallota, who was now lying partly over him, was forced up so that his thighs crashed hard against

the boards. The half-breed grunted. Then the
fingers left Catsfoot's throat under the shock of
impact, and the loss of balance caused by the angle
of Catsfoot's body.

Now the main weight of Gallota was across
Catsfoot's face and his arms were threshing, trying
again to contact the throat. But, in that position, it
was impossible for him to do so. He twisted off
Catsfoot. Then, hands out, he groped again to
locate his prey.

He would have found it. His fingers would once
more have the death grip. And this time, strength
all but gone, Catsfoot would have been unable to
resist.

But for Steve . . .

Now Steve was between the ground and the
floorboards. He was much taller than Gallota and
therefore could not move so easily. And, because
his eyes were not yet adjusted to the dim light, he
could not see so clearly. But he had one big
advantage—he was fresh. He had not suffered the
shock of the first fall, he had not used any of his
strength in desperate moments of struggle.

Gallota was nearer to Steve than Catsfoot. And
Gallota, with his clawing hands, had his back to him.
Steve found that he could get into a semi-crouch
before meeting the resistance of the boards. In that
position, he made a quick crawl forward. His right
hand touched a stone and instinctively he held on to
it. Then the silhouette of the half-breed was within
reach. He sensed, rather than saw, that the maniac

could be taken by surprise. Holding the stone in the flat of his palm, he crashed it at Gallota.

There was no particular aim about it. No time to select a careful target. The stone hit Gallota between the shoulder blades. The dwarf gave a whimpering cough. He swayed sideways, raising his body a few inches. Then he collapsed at Catsfoot's side.

Steve crawled up to Catsfoot. He did not talk. Words were needless. Linking his hands under Catsfoot's armpits, he pulled gently. Because of lack of space, it was difficult and exhausting work. But somehow he got Catsfoot directly under the opening. From that moment, Catsfoot was able to help himself. Shakily, he got to his feet and stepped on to the floor, into the room where five throwing knives and an upturned table were the tokens of the beginning of a frenzied struggle.

Catsfoot's long, fair hair was smothered with dust. His face was streaked with dirt. And at the front of his throat two ugly pink patches showed. Steve put the table upright and Catsfoot sat wearily on the edge of it.

"Thanks, son. I'd never have got out of that if it hadn't been for you."

But Steve ignored the compliment. He was feeling Catsfoot's left arm and right hand. When he had finished, he gave a sigh of relief.

"They don't seem to have taken any extra damage," he said.

"I'm all right—but we'd better see to Gallota."

"What are you going to do with him, Catsfoot?"

"Right now, we'll have to get him out from under the floor. He can't stay there."

"And then . . . ?"

"Then nothing," Catsfoot said, "except we may have to put those knives where he can't find them. I'll know later about that."

"But we can't let him stay here—he's capable of anything!"

"Sure he is—but only because he's scared of everybody. I figure we can find a way of keeping him here without harming him."

"But does it matter if we *do* harm him? Hang it, he tried to kill us! He's crazy!"

"Yep, he's crazy. That's why I don't hold him responsible for anything he's done. Remember, he's a half-breed—part white, part Indian. Those people have to take the worst of everything. Indians don't want them and neither do the whites. They're all on their own. I guess that's enough to turn any man's mind. We've got to be grateful it isn't you or me."

This was not the first time that Steve had been surprised by Catsfoot's humanity, by his compassion. He had first seen it in the canyon, when he had risked his life to protect Apache prisoners. Now he was seeing it again. Catsfoot was a merciless enemy of those who deliberately chose the paths of brutality and tyranny. But he was quick to understand those misfortunes which sometimes twisted men into something which was a parody of their true selves. Steve understood anew why this trail scout, who could probably draw and shoot faster and straighter than any man alive, hated to be known as a gun-fighter. His guns were a necessary tool of his trade at a time when the new territories were a cauldron of hatred and violence. Without them, he could not remain alive and neither could he protect those who entrusted their safety to him. But in his heart, he loathed killing and despised even the threat of force.

"I think I understand what you mean," Steve said slowly.

"I'm glad you do, son. A lot of blood's been shed in the past few days, and I feel that we haven't seen the end of it. But I don't aim to make a sacrifice out of a man who never did have any kind of chance . . ."

At that moment there came a scraping sound from under the floor. They waited, watching the opening. Presently Gallota crawled out of it.

Now he seemed even smaller. Even more shrunken. The hatred was still there, smouldering in his pit-like eyes. But fear was present, too. It showed as he glanced at Steve, then let his eyes rest on Catsfoot. He backed away from both of them, only stopping when he was against a far wall. Then the little pink tongue came out, darting round the lips.

"Well . . . you're goin' to kill me, so don't wait! Get it over!" His words came huskily.

Catsfoot was still sitting on the corner of the table as he said: "We're not going to kill you, Gallota. We'll not harm you in any way, so relax."

The half-breed gave a disbelieving smile. "Who d'you think you talk to? Y'think I like that kind of talk? I tried to finish you and failed. Now you finish me! Mebbe I'm scared, but I won't crawl for mercy!"

"There's no need for you to crawl to anyone," Catsfoot told him in his quiet way. "We didn't mean any harm to you when we came here and things haven't changed. All we want is to rest up for a few days."

Gallota looked away from Catsfoot, his face confused. He was staring through the empty window frame when he said: "You are crazy enough to give me another chance to fix you?"

"That depends on you, Gallota. Mebbe you were scared of us when we came here, or mebbe you just had a lot of grudges you wanted to work off. Whatever the reason, it's done with now. There's plenty of room for the three of us in Karlsbergh."

Gallota shrugged his shoulders. "Okay. It seems like you've gone soft, Catsfoot. Mebbe you're scared to fix me . . ." Suddenly the old fury returned. He broke off, then shouted: "But I'll get you . . . you and the kid! Mebbe you'll try to keep my knives away from me, but I'll get round that! I'll save the Brogans the trouble of . . ."

Catsfoot interrupted quietly. "No need to look for a chance to kill me," he said. "You can do it right now, if you feel that way." He kicked one of the knives along the floor. It stopped at Gallota's feet. "Pick it up," he said.

Gallota stared for long seconds at the blade. Then at Steve. His lips parted in a snarl.

"A nice trap, just to make it look right! The kid has one of your guns. He'll shoot just as soon as I try to . . ."

Again Catsfoot cut in. This time, he spoke to Steve. "Put that gun on the table," he ordered.

"But we'll . . ."

"Just do like I say, Steve."

Unwillingly, Steve obeyed. But he remained at the table until Catsfoot said: "Stand at the other end of the room." His steps dragging, Steve did that.

Then Catsfoot turned again to Gallota. "We're helpless," he said. "You can pick up that knife and put it into me any time you choose. If that's what you want to do, get on with it."

Gallota's face twitched. "Folks say I'm mad," he muttered. "I figure I'm not alone. Okay . . . if that's the way you want it . . ." He bent down and grasped the blade of the knife.

The familiar stance returned—the weapon balanced delicately between his fingers. "Where'll you have it, Catsfoot? I can put it any place you want."

Catsfoot said in his quiet way: "You won't put it anywhere, Gallota. You won't throw that knife. You don't kill men who can't hit back."

Slowly Catsfoot began to move towards Gallota. Sweat stood on the half-breed's forehead. He shouted: "Don't come any nearer! One more step and I'll put the steel into you!"

But Catsfoot kept on advancing, without hurry, and without any sign of fear. The knife quivered in Gallota's hand. The wrist pulsated, on the point of making the fatal flick. But it was as though the muscles were held in bondage, as though the physical part of the half-breed was trying to make the throw, but was being held in check by another force.

Then Catsfoot halted—only a few inches from him.

"No need to throw the knife now," Catsfoot said. "You can push it into me—if you feel that way."

Gallota breathed: "You're mighty sure I won't do it!"

"Of course I'm sure."

"Why?"

"Because I wouldn't kill you. I could have had you killed just a minute back. I figure you feel just about the same way about these things as I do. You ain't a willing murderer, Gallota."

The black depth of Gallota's eyes stared un-blinkingly into those of Catsfoot. The blade slid between his fingers until they held the hilt. His arm came back, swinging behind his waist. He was poised for an upward stabbing thrust.

"You've been kiddin' yourself!" he said. "I *am* a killer! This is where you collect . . . !"

Catsfoot did not move. His eyes were still fixed on those of the half-breed. Gallota brought the knife forward and up. But he did so slowly. When he stopped, the point of the blade was pressing into Catsfoot's buckskins at the area under the lungs.

"Ain't you goin' to admit you're wrong about me, Catsfoot?" he asked. "Ain't you goin' to say I'm just an ordinary killer?"

Catsfoot said: "Not an ordinary killer, Gallota. Mebbe if you'd had any sort of chance, you'd never have been a killer at all."

There was a long, tense pause. Then it happened —happened with extraordinary abruptness.

Gallota threw down the knife.

He turned away from Catsfoot and walked heavily towards the window. Looking out over what had been the main street, he asked: "I am not Indian and I am not white. Does that not make me the worst of both?"

"It could make you the best of both, Gallota."

The half-breed again faced Catsfoot. "I have learned to throw a knife swifter and truer than any man," he said. "I have killed many and the law seeks me."

"You're not alone there."

"You do not sneer at me?"

"I don't sneer at anyone."

"And you do not seek vengeance on me?"

"I don't do that, either. To me, you're just a plain man and I want to forget what's happened—if you'll forget it, too."

Gallota's face changed. It lightened and something near to a smile creased it. "In all my time, I have never met one such as you," he said. "You trust me. No man has trusted me before to-day. It is good to be trusted . . . now tell me of the Brogans. I want to know why they seek you."

Catsfoot returned to the table. Again he sat on the corner of it. In a few, quick sentences he told Gallota of what had happened.

For a time after he had finished, Gallota was silent. Then he said: "I know now why you and the kid are here. But have you not wondered why I, too, have taken refuge in Karlsbergh?"

"You gave me a hint, Gallota—you said the law was after you."

"I killed a saloon keeper in Tucson. I flicked a blade into him. If the law finds me, I will hang."

"Why did you kill the saloon keeper?"

Gallota's face became heavy again. His lips became taut against his yellow teeth.

"He laughed at me! Not once, but many times. He mocked me before others in Tucson . . . he called me a dwarf . . . a half-Indian. It went on for days . . . until the hour came when I could take no more. Then I threw my knife. I rode out of the place with a marshal's posse after me. After three days my horse broke down and I came here on foot. The posse will still be seeking me, for they never give up when they are after a mad half-breed. Perhaps they will come here . . . if they do, I will fight them with my knives."

Catsfoot picked his fedora from the floor and looked at the sliced brim. "From what I know, you'd do a lot of damage against the posse," he said. "But mebbe you'd do better to give yourself up. You were provoked into throwing that knife and that would count in your favour at a trial."

"A trial! I'm a half-breed. Mebbe they wouldn't worry about that delay. They'd just string me up as soon as they caught me!"

Catsfoot did not answer. But he knew that Gallota was not exaggerating. Lynching was still popular in Arizona. Men suspected of crimes were hanged after being given, at the best, a mere mockery of a trial. They were denied the help of trained lawyers who could test the stories of accusing witnesses. They did not even have the basic right of an impartial hearing by judge and jury. In the great majority of cases, those who hanged were guilty. But, inevitably, there were times when innocent men suffered the death penalty. And such matters as provocation were seldom taken into account.

Catsfoot was still thinking about this when Gallota added: "You want to be my friend—then I am your friend. We will stay in this place together. And if the Brogan brothers ride in here before your hands are better, I and my knives will defend you!"

Catsfoot was about to reply when a whistling sound came from outside. A moment later there was a soft pattering as a suddenly gathered wind drove hard dust against the building.

"A mesa storm's on the way," Catsfoot said, looking out of the window. "It looks like it'll be a bad one—the first of the season . . ."

CHAPTER EIGHT

TEMPEST

MESA storm . . .

They came to Arizona each May and June, when rising temperatures caused atmospheric disturbances on the great plateaus. Sometimes they consisted only of high, screeching winds and hours of booming thunder, the rain being absorbed by the dry atmosphere before reaching the ground. At other times, rain fell with tropical intensity, quickly turning stone-hard earth into marshland, converting streams into torrents, rivers into inland seas.

Already, it was certain that a wet mesa was on the way, for heavy clouds were obscuring the late evening sun and the air held a sudden chill.

"We'll have to get the horses under cover," Catsfoot said. "Steve, you see to it. You know where the stables are—at the end of the street."

Steve nodded and ran outside, picking his steps carefully as he crossed the boardwalk. The wind, steadily gathering force, cut through his tunic and drove stinging dust pellets on to his face. He led the two horses at a run down the street until he came to the large building. The roof had partly collapsed. One of the walls bulged ominously outward and there was a wide gap where the double doors had

been. The place did not look as if it would survive
many more years. But to-day it would serve to protect the animals from the worst of the weather. As
he led them inside, Steve saw that the long hitching
rail remained intact. And there was a stone trough
beside it, cracked where parts of the roof had fallen.
The rain, when it came, would rapidly collect in the
trough, so the animals would not suffer thirst.

He removed the saddles and used a piece of rope
to fix a running line to the hitching rail, so that the
horses could move to the trough. He also emptied
their corn bags near them.

The place had an unpleasantly sickly smell,
caused mainly by a black pile of rotted hay which
lay in a corner. Close to the hay were the remnants
of a couple of chairs, both upturned, and a splintered
mess which had been a roll-top desk. Steve guessed
that it was there that the stable owner had kept
his business accounts.

After a last brief look round, Steve ran back
towards the assay office. He was almost there when
a streak of lightning cut through the gathering darkness. It was followed by raw thunder, then the rain.
Driven by the wind, it came down at an acute angle
and with ferocious force. The drumming of it on the
boardwalks competed with the incessant thunder.
He was shaking the wet out of his hair when he
rejoined Catsfoot and Gallota.

Gallota had produced food from a hoarded
supply—all of it pemmican. He was sharing it
equally between the three when a distant crash told

of some building which had collapsed under the gathering fury.

"This will last all night," Gallota said. "I know the signs . . . it is the worst kind of storm . . ."

Eighteen miles from the ghost town. . . .

One of the Brogans said: "It's goin' to be a real bad storm. We'll have to get under cover."

"I was thinkin' the same. How about cuttin' back to the canyon?"

"We've been there—no sense in turnin' back. That way, we'll be givin' Catsfoot extra time. We want to find him fast."

"But there ain't any other place to go."

"There's Karlsbergh."

"Karlsbergh. . . . Say, that place must've fallen flat by this time."

"Mebbe most of it has, but there must still be a few buildings to give us shelter. We can be there in a few hours."

The Brogan brothers looked at each other. Then, without a further word, they pressed spurs and rode through the gathering storm, towards Karlsbergh.

Catsfoot was dozing on the floor of the assay office. Sleep would not come to him because of the throbbing pain in his left arm and a dull ache which had recently developed in his right hand. He lay in a corner, only partly shielded from the fierce air currents which swirled through the open doorways and between the gaping cracks in walls and roof.

Mostly as he lay there, he wondered about the people from the canyon. If all was going well, they ought to be very near Fort Coulter. In fact, because rain must be quickening the flow of the river, it was possible that those on the rafts had already reached safety. He was considering that chance when his eyes suddenly opened. He stared into the darkness, listening. Then he kicked his blanket aside. Awkwardly, he sat upright, ears still straining.

The movement awakened Steve and Gallota. There was a splutter of light as the half-breed lit a candle and found a place for it away from the worst of the draughts. Steve asked: "What's the matter, Catsfoot? The pain getting worse?"

Catsfoot shook his head. "I'm not sure, but I thought I heard horses moving about the town."

Gallota rubbed his eyes and yawned. "You make a mistake," he said confidently. "No one can hear anything above the noise of this storm. A thousand horses could stampede through Karlsbergh right now and we wouldn't hear them."

Catsfoot looked doubtful. "Mebbe . . . but my ears are good. Anyway, I'd like to be sure. I guess I'll take a look around."

Steve stood up. "You're not going out in this storm," he said. "Mebbe you won't admit it, but you'll be a sick man till the time comes to take those bandages off. I'll look m'self."

Catsfoot hesitated. Then he said: "Okay, take a quick look round the town stables, because if I *did* hear hoofs, that's where they came from. Our horses could have broken loose."

"I won't be long," Steve said, picking up a spare blanket from Gallota's pile. He clutched it over his head and shoulders as he left the building. Immediately, the wind hit him like a blow from a battering ram. It pushed him back a few steps before, bent almost double, he was able to move towards the far end of the town. Then he remembered that he had not brought a gun. He decided against going back, since it seemed unlikely that anyone was around. And they had even less reason to expect trouble so soon after their arrival.

The full moon was almost entirely obscured by thick cloud, so that there was little light as Steve splashed through deep pools which had formed in the street. Between those pools, the once-baked earth had been transformed into a glue-like bog. Within seconds the driven rain had soaked his blanket, tunic and breeches.

He felt relieved when he saw the shadowy mass of the stables. Head down, he made for the entrance, hand groping for a tin of sulphur matches in his pocket. Then, almost inside the sagging walls, he halted. A faint splash of yellow light was coming from within the stables. He heard voices, too. Familiar voices which speeded his pulse, brought a hot dryness to his throat, momentarily turned his brain into a paralysed mush.

Recovering from the first shock, he turned to run back to the assay office. But he halted after a couple of steps. He could be mistaken. They *sounded* like the Brogans, but . . .

Steve knew that he must look and be sure.

Slowly he returned. He had to gather all his nerve before he could force himself to take a cautious peep into the building.

In the light of a kerosene lamp, the Brogans were standing beside the horses belonging to Catsfoot and Steve. Their own animals had been tethered a little distance away. Both men were grinning.

". . . and to think we might never have come to this dead town if it hadn't been for the storm," one of them was saying.

"Yep—it sure does show things come right for straight dealin' hombres like us!"

They laughed—that humourless, grating parody. Then: "I suppose there ain't no doubt this is Catsfoot's hoss?"

"Sure it's his. I remember it. And the other's the one the kid was ridin'."

"They'll be asleep right now, we might as well fix 'em and have it over."

The other shook his head. "That can wait till daylight when the storm's blown out and we've rested. They can't get away—not if we bunk down right here close to their hosses. And it'll be kinda nice to see Catsfoot's face when we pick our own time to move up on him . . . y'know, we'll be able to have fun with that critter before we put a slug into him. I figure we can make him whine, now he can't draw them guns of his."

"I guess you're right. No sense in goin' out into the storm again . . ."

Steve watched them move away to the distant end of the stables, seeking a place to sleep. They chose the pile of rotted hay, pulling some of the vile-smelling stuff down and smoothing it with their boots. Then, the lamp still burning, they unfastened their gun belts, took off their wet jackets, sprawled on their backs. They mumbled to each other for a short time, but Steve could not hear the words. Eventually, their eyes closed and they began to breath deeply and regularly. They were asleep.

Now Steve's brain was clear. Carefully, he went over the facts. If he simply returned to warn Catsfoot, what could Catsfoot do? Nothing. His gun hands useless, he would be completely helpless. And, as one of the Brogans had said, he could not get away, for it would be impossible to get the horses out of the stable.

But what of Gallota, their new friend?

Gallota had pledged himself to defend Catsfoot with his knives. Perhaps Gallota would want to come to the stables. If so, he might be able to use those awful blades of his before the Brogans had a chance to open their eyes. Perhaps . . . but one thing was certain—Catsfoot would never allow that. He would never approve the killing of two sleeping men, even the Brogans. And even though it were his only chance of survival.

That meant that when the Brogans came out, Steve would have to try to outshoot them. But immediately he realised that the mere idea was ridiculous. He would have no chance at all against those top-guns. They could fill him with lead before he even took first pressure on the trigger. Certainly Gallota would do a lot better. Against even odds, the half-caste might even come off best. But two to one . . . His life and Steve's would be sacrificed for nothing. And Catsfoot would still die.

Suppose the Brogans could be disarmed as they slept? If he, Steve, could get their guns away from them?

As the idea occurred to him, Steve knew that he must attempt to carry it through. If he failed? Well, things could not be made any worse.

Carefully he moved into the stables, pressing against the wall.

The Brogans lay about thirty feet from him. There was no cover at this side of the building. If either of the Brogans awoke, he would be seen immediately. He wondered whether to slip over to the other side where the horses were tethered, using the cover of their bodies and of the stone trough. He decided against that, for his presence might frighten the animals and rouse the two men. There was nothing for it—he must attempt a direct approach.

Still keeping his back to the sagging wall, he moved sideways. One careful, gentle step, then a palpitating halt. Followed by another step, another halt . . . And his eyes never left the faces of the two brothers.

He covered half the distance. A horse whinnied and stamped. It was Catsfoot's and, head turned against halter, it had recognised Steve. That was a possibility which Steve had not foreseen. Both the Brogans stirred slightly. They would have done no more than that, but for the fact that the animal whinnied again. Steve took the only chance. He threw himself flat on the stone floor, folded arms covering his face. He remained there, completely motionless, praying that in the dim light from the lantern, he would not be seen.

He heard a cough and a faint rustling. Without seeing, he knew that one of the Brogans was sitting upright. Then silence. Silence which created agony by the second. And second piled on second, agony on agony. Steve waited for the shout which would tell him that he had been seen, for the hot slug which would cut into his flesh.

A voice said: "Why can't that hoss keep quiet?"

The question was followed by another faint rustling and a yawn. Steve squinted over his folded arms. The Brogans seemed to be sleeping again.

Partly because he was shaking under nervous strain, partly to give them both a chance to settle again, Steve waited on the ground for at least five minutes. Then, inch by inch, he got to his feet and resumed his crablike walk. Catsfoot's horse was still watching him. But he was less worried about it now, for if it should whinny again the Brogans were not likely to pay much attention after one false alarm.

As he drew closer, he gained a desperate confidence. Now those sprawling figures were almost within an arm stretch. Their gun belts and holsters lay between them. A quick dive, perhaps . . .

Yes, that might succeed. But Steve remembered how fast those brothers could move. And it would not be entirely simple to lift the guns from their holsters. Because they were lying loose, it would be necessary to hold each holster with one hand while removing the gun from it with the other. That would take precious time—too long for safety. Another approach must be found.

Pausing, Steve inspected the mound of rotted hay. It was piled to a height of four feet against the far wall. The Brogans were sprawled slightly to one side of it. It ought to be possible to crawl round the back of it to the Brogans. The hay would deaden any sound of movement. And, while lying flat, he could remove the guns, then move out, without their knowing what had happened. Yes, that certainly offered the best chance. If luck stayed with him, he might manage it . . .

Steve lowered himself to his hands and knees and crawled on to the rotting pile. Here the stench was sickening and the black stuff wound itself round his fingers and legs. As he crept further over it, he sank deep until he was almost covered. That made progress difficult, but it also concealed him completely. When he felt the wall, Steve turned in the mass of hay. It was as he had hoped. He emerged directly behind the Brogans. Their heads were less than two feet from him. Their guns were scarcely a yard away.

Now to remove those guns.

There was a temptation to snatch, to get it over. He resisted it, and in the dim light he carefully gauged the position of each butt as it showed out of its holster. One was slightly closer than the other, but the cartridge-filled belt had fallen loosely over it. Before it could be removed, that belt would have to be lifted clear. There did not seem to be any particular difficulty about that, except for the fact that, the belt being heavy, it must be handled with care. If he allowed any part of it to drop, it would make a distinct thud.

The Brogans were still breathing regularly.

Inch by torturing inch, Steve eased himself forward, until his head was between those of the Brogans. Then he stretched out his hands—slowly, infinitely gently.

The fingers of his right hand touched the ebony of the butt. His left hand took a grip on the belt, lifted it clear.

Now . . .

But now his arms would not move.

They were paralysed. And at the same time they were being crushed, as though the bones were being pressed to powder. The powerful hands of the Brogans were encircling his forearm. Savage, pitiless faces were grinning at him.

"You don't catch us that way," one of them was saying. "We saw you when the hoss whinnied! It

was kinda funny just to lie back and see what you'd
try to do . . ."

Catsfoot said: "Dawn's breaking. Steve's been
a heck of a time. Reckon I'll see what he's doing."

Gallota shook his wizened little head. "I'll go.
I am a dwarf mebbe, but my hands are good. If
there is any trouble, I know what to do."

"Okay—seeing I'm just useless right now. I
guess I shouldn't have let him go out—but even if
I had heard right, I didn't figure on anything more
than our horses snapping their halters because they
were scared . . . now I'm wondering . . ."

Gallota pushed his five unsheathed knives into his
belt. "I think mebbe Steve is just trying to round
your hosses up," he said. "But I will take my
blades—just in case."

His tiny figure darted out of the room.

The Brogans checked the knots of the rope which
lashed Steve's hands behind his back. Then one of
them pushed a filthy square of cloth into his mouth
and secured it with a length of cord.

"That'll keep you outa trouble till we've fixed
Catsfoot. Then we'll come back and attend to you.
We want it to be a nice surprise for Catsfoot, findin'
us here. If we put a slug into you right now, he
might hear it. So you'll wait, kid. But don't worry
—you won't wait long."

One of them gave him a push. He fell on his back.
Staring frantically up, he watched the Brogans put

on their gun belts. And, side by side, they walked out of the stables, without taking another glance at him.

Steve tried to think of some way of freeing himself, of warning Catsfoot and Gallota. But, as he lay there writhing, he knew that he would never get out of those bonds. If he had obeyed his first instinct by running back to the assay office when he saw the Brogans, something *might* have been done. But now it was all hopeless. Catsfoot would die. If Gallota's friendship proved more than mere talk, then he too would perish. Then Steve's own turn would come.

Steve turned his head to the ground, not wanting to see or hear anything, not even wanting to think.

The storm had passed. It vanished as quickly as it came. The thunder rapidly became more distant until it faded utterly. The lightning lost its venom before going altogether. And the driving rain departed with the dark clouds.

The newly rising sun brought a fierce light on the broken buildings, black with wetness, and on the pools and mud of the main street. Already, wisps of steam were rising. Before midday, the ghost town of Karlsbergh would be sweltering in torrid, damp heat.

The Brogans walked into the centre of the street, taking a careful look at the town.

"Guess we'll have to search every framewood in the place," one of them said.

"Nope—Catsfoot will have laid up in one of the places without too many holes in the walls, and there's not so many of those. We'll just take a look at the best buildings."

Slithering slightly on the mud, they began walking slowly along the street. Together they noticed the assay office, which was some distance away.

"That place don't look so bad. Better than any of the others. Guess we'll go there first."

They quickened their pace, faces alert with expectancy.

Then they halted.

A dwarf of a half-breed had appeared from behind the ruin of a carpenter's shop. A shrivelled man whose yellow teeth were bared like those of an animal on the hunt. In one of his hands he held a weighted throwing knife. He had taken up a stance directly opposite them, in the centre of the street.

"Good morning," the little man said.

"Who in tarnation are you?"

"Gallota. And you?"

"That don't concern you none, but we're the Brogans. Mebbe that name means enough for you to keep out of our way. And if you value that rotten brown skin of yours, you'd best put your knife in your belt."

Gallota continued to balance the knife between his fingers.

"You looking for someone?" he asked.

"Yep—a tall hombre name of Catsfoot. If you've been in this place long, you'll have seen him."

"I've seen him," answered Gallota quietly.

"Then do yourself some good by showing us where he's hidin' out . . . and put that knife away, like I told you."

More of Gallota's teeth showed. In those ebony eyes there was almost a thoughtful expression.

"You goin' to harm Catsfoot?" he asked in words of silk.

"We're gonna kill him."

Gallota gave a short twist of thumb and forefinger. The knife jumped from his right hand to his left. Another almost casual flick and it returned to the right hand. Then he said: "I am the fastest man alive with my blades."

"Mebbe you are—but a knife don't travel as quick as a slug, so don't get ideas."

"But you don't understand . . . Catsfoot is my friend. He is my only friend. I have never had a friend before and I do not want to lose him."

The Brogans glanced at each other. "You're crazy," one of them said. "If you want to get y'self rubbed out, that's okay by us. It'll spoil the surprise for Catsfoot, but we'll fix him just the same. You got one last chance to get out of our way, you filthy half-Injun runt! Move! Or you stop a slug!"

The blade left Gallota's hand. There was a sound somewhere between a hiss and a whistle as it spun through the air, bright steel and dull haft intermingling in a blur of colour.

It was still travelling, still in its death-laden

flight, when Karlsbergh reverberated to the cruel crash of the Brogans' guns.

Gallota took a few weird, dancing steps backwards. At the same time, he groped frantically to get another knife out of his belt, struggled to throw yet again. He got a weak grip on the hilt. Then the fingers relaxed. They fell nerveless to his side. Gallota knew that he was dying. But some men die hard. They squeeze the last fragment of fight out of a flickering and fading heart. Gallota, the half-breed, was such a man.

He dropped on his stomach, legs in a pool, head in the churned mud. He tried to crawl, tried to force himself towards the Brogans. He managed a few inches. That was all.

In the moment before he died, he rolled on to his stomach and wondered why the sky was black.

But Gallota had not died alone.

A blade was deep in the chest of one of the Brogans. Deep to the hilt. He, too, was in the mud of the main street. Lying within inches of Gallota. And just as still as Gallota . . .

His brother stood over him, staring at him, face twitching under the compulsion of fury. He stayed like that for a short time. Then, holding his smoking gun level with his waist, he moved towards the assay office, towards Catsfoot.

Those reverberating shots . . .
They brought Catsfoot to the outer door of the assay office. Then he saw them—saw the two who

Brogan moved towards the assay office, towards
Catsfoot.

had died, and the Brogan who had survived, who was coming for him, gun cocked and held ready.

Catsfoot drew back into the office, moving behind the counter. He tried to move his left arm, to shift it in its sling. The perpetual pain seared into agony which made him groan. That was still completely useless. But what of his right hand? Steve had said that the wound there was much less serious, just a torn muscle beneath the thumb. Perhaps . . .

He raised the bandages to his lips . . . with his teeth, he tore at the knots. They were tight, difficult to wrench free. He could hear an approaching squelch of feet on the mud. Getting near—very near. Confident, unhesitating steps of a man sure of his victim.

At last, the knots began to slip. With a final tug, Catsfoot got them free. A few whirls of his wrist, and the wounded hand was uncovered.

The furrowed wound was still open and raw. Catsfoot gave another groan as he attempted to move the thumb. It was as stiff and as powerless as clay. And he could only bend his trigger finger with difficulty. There was little strength in it—certainly not nearly enough to exert the pull necessary to fire a Peacemaker.

Now the footsteps were on the boardwalk.

Catsfoot retreated to the inner room. Stepping over blankets which still lay on the boards, he paused for a fraction of time at the edge of the jagged hole in the floor. He dropped into it. Quickly he stretched out, so that his body was under the boards, his head directly beneath the hole. Breathing hard because of spasms of pain, he hooked his semi-useless forefinger into the trigger guard and lifted the right-hand gun out of its holster. He laid the barrel on the edge of the hole, facing the door.

Brogan was in the building now. Catsfoot could hear him advancing across the office, feet grinding on the broken glass which had covered the portrait of Lincoln. Catsfoot raised his head so that his eyes were above the edge of the flooring. Then he tried for the one slender chance of being able to use his gun. One finger was not strong enough to pull the trigger, therefore two must be used. He tried to force his first and second fingers into the trigger guard. But the Peacemaker was not designed for this. There was not sufficient space, unless . . .

After a first futile attempt, Catsfoot put both fingers in his mouth, wetting them thoroughly. Lubrication made the vital difference. This time both fingers got into position—but only at the cost of another spasm of acute agony as he used all his strength to force them there.

Brogan had not yet appeared. The sound of his footfalls had ceased. It could be that he, a veteran of scores of gun fights, sensed danger. Catsfoot heard him cough, the sound coming starkly clear through the thin inner wall.

"You there, Catsfoot?" The voice was slightly uncertain, in the way of a person who feels that he may be speaking in an empty building. Catsfoot remained silent, two fingers on the trigger and the weight of his Peacemaker resting on the edge of the hole. Only the top part of his head showed, the rest of him concealed under the floor.

Brogan spoke again. "If you're hidin', Catsfoot, it won't do you no good. I'm comin' to fix you! I'm comin' right now . . . !"

Catsfoot heard another heavy pace. At the same time, he aimed at the centre of the doorway and began to pull on the trigger. He *had* to aim before the target was there, *had* to begin to fire before there was anything to fire at. That was the one hope he had of getting in the first slug.

The brother appeared.

Suddenly he was standing under the door lintel, massive, brutal, exuding vicious power. But he was not in the centre of the opening. Not where Catsfoot had hoped he would be, not where Catsfoot had managed to take clumsy aim with his Peacemaker. He was standing well to the side of the opening, almost against one of the warped doorposts. And his eyes were flickering round the room, momentarily puzzled.

The hammer of the Peacemaker was almost at the end of its backward travel. In a fraction of a second it would drop on the cap and explode the cartridge. And the bullet would miss by a clear foot. . . .

Catsfoot made a desperate attempt to correct his aim. It was a matter of turning the barrel a mere half-inch to the right—something which in the ordinary way he would do instinctively. But now his all but useless hand was incapable of fine judgment. To some degree, he had to rely on luck.

In the last infinitesimal fragment of time before the hammer fell, Brogan saw Catsfoot. And Brogan's gun, held at his waist, was ready cocked. But no one can react immediately to what he sees. There must always be a lapse, however minute, while the brain flashes messages to the nerves and nerves move the muscles.

That was why, although both guns seemed to crash out simultaneously, Catsfoot's bullet was there first. It went into Brogan's right shoulder. It was not a fatal wound, but it was a disabling one.

And, because he could only see part of Catsfoot's head, Brogan's aim was also out. More seriously out than Catsfoot's. His slug caused a white streak to appear in the wood at Catsfoot's side before vanishing under the floor.

Brogan's gun was falling from his hand. He was staring at Catsfoot in a confused and stupid way. He opened his mouth as if to speak, but at first only a hiss of pain emerged.

Then three words emerged. Whimpering, pleading words.

"Don't touch me . . ." he said.

As he spoke, he collapsed on to the rotting boards.

He dropped slowly, clutching a wounded shoulder. And he was sobbing, sobbing because of pain, fear, and the knowledge of utter defeat.

Catsfoot emerged from the hole which he and

Gallota had made. He moved swiftly towards Brogan and the gunslinger cringed away. But Catsfoot did not so much as glance at him. He stepped round the man, then broke into a run as he made for the town stables.

Steve and Catsfoot came slowly out of those stables, leading their horses. Almost immediately they stopped. The main street was much as it had been in the last few desolate years. Save for the two bodies which lay as a grim token of the day's gun and knife battle. And save for the five Apaches who were sitting their ponies only a few yards from the assay office. Like monuments, they sat, tall, straight, proudly arrogant. And they were gazing at Catsfoot. The Apache in the centre was holding a battle lance and he wore a wide, doeskin band round his forehead. It was Earo.

Earo kneed the sides of his pony and, leaving the others, he trotted towards Catsfoot and Steve. He reined in when within easy talking distance of them. With unblinking, expressionless eyes, he stared at Catsfoot. Then he said: "Only one of the brothers is dead."

Catsfoot said: "That's right."

"The other is wounded—but he lives."

Catsfoot nodded. Earo continued: "So . . . you have not fulfilled the bond. You remember the pact we made? If your life and that of the boy are to be spared, *both* of the brothers must die."

"That is so," Catsfoot said. "I'm not going to

argue about it . . . I guess it'd be a waste of time, anyway."

"It is good that you speak thus, for it means you will not cry out against my justice." Catsfoot did not reply. So after hesitating, Earo added: "You have been watched by my braves from the time you left us. So have the brothers. I have heard of all that has happened, except for two things we could not see—how did you, with your maimed hands, slay one of the brothers with a knife and wound the other?"

"I didn't use the knife," Catsfoot said. "Gallota did that. . . ."

"Gallota!" Earo repeated the name quickly. Then he moved his horse towards the tiny body which lay in the mud. He looked at it for many long moments. When he returned, he said: "I know of Gallota. He could use his knives faster than any man and with them he slew many men. For that I have never condemned him. But he could never walk among my people, for he was half white. His blood was bad and it is good that he is dead."

Catsfoot's eyes narrowed. "If you're going to blame him for his blood, don't forget that half of it is Indian! There was a lot of good in that man, but it never had a chance to come out—anyway, not till the end! Mebbe the best in him was Indian, or mebbe it was white—I don't care about that. But I do know he died to save Steve and me, and if I hear you talk just one more word against him, I'll . . ."

"What will you do?" Earo interrupted softly.

Catsfoot held up his lacerated right hand. "I've got this. It's not much use, but I'll try to use it for one last shot—a shot at you, Earo!"

"You will do that if I again speak ill of the half-breed?"

"I will!"

Earo shrugged. Then he levelled his lance until the point of it was no more than a foot from Catsfoot's chest. Deliberately, he said: "My words will test you . . ."

Steve shouted: "Don't try to draw, Catsfoot! You can't do it and he'll kill you with the lance!"

"He's going to kill both of us anyway," Catsfoot said. Then looking at Earo, he added: "Go on. What were you thinking of saying about Gallota?"

"He had tainted blood and . . ."

Catsfoot's right hand streaked for his holster. Most—but not all—of the old speed was there. But it was when he tried to grip the butt, when he tried to draw, that his helplessness was revealed. Inch by inch, his face turning pale with pain, he lifted the Peacemaker free. But his injured hand would not grip it. The gun fell between his feet.

And Earo. . . .

Earo's lance was now pressing against Catsfoot's buckskin jacket. And he was saying: "You did not hear me to the end. I will finish my words about Gallota."

"I don't want to hear them! Get your work over! Put your lance through me!"

But Earo did not move the lance. "Gallota's

blood was tainted," he said, "yet his was the noble heart of a mountain eagle, within him was the spirit of a warrior. These things I know now, because he died for you, and you are a good man—yes, I say you are good, even though you are white and my enemy!"

The lance was withdrawn from Catsfoot's chest. . . .

And suddenly Earo was smiling. "We also are warriors, you and I," he was saying. "Our skins are different and the story of our peoples is being told in tears and pain. Yet we respect each other. So I say it is good that you and the boy shall live. The time may come when we will fight again—and we shall show no mercy to each other. But this day we part in peace." He paused, half-turned and pointed his lance towards the assay office. "You can take the brother who is there to Fort Coulter. The other brother is also wounded and with my people. We will send him to the fort, so that both may face white justice. I have spoken. . . ."

Earo turned his pony. He cantered back to the four other Apaches. And he raised his lance in a salute before riding out of the ghost town.

Minutes passed. During them, Catsfoot and Steve stood very still, watching the Indians until they had vanished from sight. Then Catsfoot said slowly: "I hope it'll never happen . . . it'll never be my wish if it does happen."

Steve looked at him curiously.

"What d'you mean, Catsfoot?"

"I mean about Earo and me fighting again. There's no call for it. Remember what Earo said about him and me respecting each other? That's true—it's something that's just happened because in a strange sort of way we've got to know each other. It *could* be the same with all Apaches and all whites. Mebbe one day it will."

Steve picked up Catsfoot's gun, knocked mud off the barrel and cylinder, then returned it to the right holster. He said: "It ain't going to be easy. Not while we've folks like the Brogans in the territory, and while a lot of the Apaches like fighting just for the sake of it."

Catsfoot nodded. "Talking of the Brogans, we've got one of them to collect. Let's do it, and get started for the fort. I sure am anxious to know whether the others have got there safe."

Still leading their horses, they walked along the street, sometimes slithering on the steaming mud. They hitched the animals to the post outside the assay office. Catsfoot hesitated. Then he put his torn right hand on the butt of his Peacemaker. He drew it slowly.

"Expecting more trouble?" Steve asked, slightly surprised.

"Could be."

"But that Brogan's wounded—you told me."

"I hit him in the shoulder and that needn't be too serious. And I've just remembered I didn't take his gun away. It dropped to the floor and I left it there."

"Left him with a gun! But that—that was just crazy!"

"I figure it was. But I had something else on my mind at that time. Something mighty important."

"What?"

"You, Steve. I wanted to get to the stables just as fast as I could because I didn't know what'd happened to you."

Suddenly Steve felt ashamed.

"Gee, I'm sorry . . . you'd never have left him with a gun if it hadn't been for me."

"I guess I wouldn't. But there's no sense in worrying about that now. You're okay and that matters to me a lot. Now we've got to collect the prisoner and I don't plan to give him any chance to pull a fast move on me."

Catsfoot leading, they moved carefully over the rotted boardwalk. The door was wide open, but Catsfoot did not enter immediately. Instead, he glanced through the gap between the hinges. A man could conceal himself behind that door. But no one was there.

Now Catsfoot was moving with those strange, gliding steps of his. Making no sound whatever. Almost as if there was a cushion of air between his saddle boots and the floor. Steve recalled that it had been like this when they had first entered the assay office, only the day before. And once again, he tried to follow Catsfoot's steps, tried to be as quiet as he. Again, it was useless. His own boots made some noise. No man could move with the eerie silence of Catsfoot, just as no man could draw and shoot like him. . . . Abruptly, Steve realised that it would have been better for both of them if he had remained outside until Catsfoot had located and covered the brother. But it was too late to do anything about that now.

The outer office was empty.

They moved through the gap at the far end of the counter, skirted the shattered glass from the lithograph of Lincoln, paused just short of the inner doorway. There Catsfoot's whole body became tense, his eyes became mere slits. Heavy seconds went by. Then he grunted and turned to Steve.

"That Brogan's gone," he said. "He must have climbed out of a window, because he'd have been seen if he'd used the boardwalk."

Steve made a baffled gesture towards the living room.

"But how can you know? We haven't been in there yet?"

"If he'd been here I'd have heard him breathing. Look for yourself."

Together, they advanced through the doorway. Catsfoot was right. The place was as Catsfoot had left it—still with the jagged hole in the floor, still with the raw streaks where bullets had scarred the woodwork. But Brogan had gone. So had the gun which he had dropped.

"He can't get far," Steve said. "Not without a horse."

"He'll try to get a horse, that's for sure. I figure

he's been watching us and he'll cut back to the stables. Remember, his own horse is still there—so we've got to move fast!"

Steve was leading as they turned and re-crossed the outer office. He stepped out of the comparative gloom of the building and on to the board-walk.

Then it happened. . . .

Then Steve suddenly stopped. He had to stop. A jab of pain smote the centre of his stomach, making him struggle for breath.

It was caused by a gun. The barrel was thrust hard into his body, just above the belt. The hammer was cocked. A thick forefinger was curled menacingly round the trigger, exerting first pressure on it. It was the finger of the Brogan brother.

There he must have taken up his position while Steve and Catsfoot were in the building—there, pressed against the outer wall. Waiting for them to come out.

Catsfoot. . . .

He had been a bare half pace behind Steve and slightly to one side of him. He was on the board-walk a fraction of a moment after the gun was pushed into Steve's stomach. Catsfoot's own gun was still in his right hand. But right now it was a useless gun—useless to help Steve. Brogan made that clear when he spoke to Catsfoot. His words came in a grating whisper, strained with desperation and hate.

"Don't try anything!" he was saying. "Don't . . .

Mebbe you can kill me, but I'll get the kid at the same time. If you want the kid to live, just do like I say. You can start by dropping that Colt of yours. . . ."

His eyes were wild, glaring. Sweat was streaming down his unshaven cheeks. Drying blood showed through the material over his right shoulder. But obviously the wound that Catsfoot had inflicted was not serious, for he could still use the hand to hold his gun. Probably the slug had done little more than tear the surface flesh. The first shock of it had naturally made him drop the gun—but now he had almost fully recovered.

"Drop your Colt!" Brogan repeated. "There won't be a second chance!"

Catsfoot had no choice—not unless he was prepared to see Steve die. His gun fell to the boardwalk.

Brogan gave a nod of satisfaction. "That's a whole lot better. Now get this—I'm ridin' out of here and I'm takin' the kid with me! When I'm well clear of this territory I'll let the kid go. But if you try to follow me, Catsfoot, I'll put a slug into him. Get it? You ain't takin' me to Fort Coulter or any other place. If I so much as catch sight of you after I leave this place, this kid'll collect. So you'd best forget about him, Catsfoot . . . !"

Steve was looking at Catsfoot and their eyes met. Steve wanted to speak, to say anything. But he could find no words. In Catsfoot's weary and pain-racked face there was a fury which matched that of

Brogan. Suddenly he was saying: "Do like he tells you, Steve. Don't try anything because it won't work out right. We're trapped, son, and we've both got to do just as Brogan tells us."

Brogan gave Steve a push. "Get on one of them hosses," he said, "and start ridin' north. Don't forget, I'll be close behind you."

For a wild second Steve thought of defying him, of deliberately electing to die so that Brogan would not get away. But almost immediately he realised the stark truth—that if he did so, Catsfoot would almost certainly perish as well. For Catsfoot would not be able to retrieve his gun in time. Not with his cruelly injured hand. Then a vital question occurred to Steve. Why was Brogan letting Catsfoot live? Once Catsfoot had dropped his gun, it would have been simple for Brogan to fire at him—to have got rid of his most dangerous enemy.

The answer came while Steve was getting unwillingly into the saddle. Brogan was standing beside the other horse. He turned to Catsfoot and said: "Y'can ride to Fort Coulter—alone. And when y'get there, tell 'em I don't want no soldiers or lawmen on my trail, neither. If I so much as smell a bluecoat, the kid'll suffer. Y'can persuade 'em to keep away from me and if you value the kid's life, you'll do just that!"

There it was! Catsfoot's life was being spared so that he could spread the warning that neither troopers nor sheriffs' posses must attempt to arrest Brogan! He, Steve, was to be used as a living shield while Brogan rode hundreds of miles into territory where he was unknown.

Catsfoot did not answer, but his eyes spoke for him. They were chips of ice as he stared at Brogan. He was wounded, he was unarmed. Yet somehow Steve sensed that the trail scout had never been more dangerous than now. Brogan must have sensed it, too, for there was an uneasy undertone to his voice as he threatened: "Don't try nothin', Catsfoot! I want you to live just so y'can get that message around. But if I *have* to finish you, I won't break my heart about it because . . ."

He ceased talking. He turned and stared hard towards the far end of the street.

Suddenly all three of them were looking in that direction. Hoof beats could be heard. The steady rhythm of several horses ridden at a gentle trot. They could not be seen yet, being hidden by a slight bend of the derelict buildings of the main street. But there could be no doubt that they were riding directly for the ghost town. And they would appear in view within a minute.

Steve muttered: "Who are they?"

That question was in Catsfoot's and Brogan's mind, also. It was unlikely that they were Apaches, for Earo and his braves had only just departed. Then who would want to ride into the place?

Brogan made a fast decision. He rapped at Steve: "We're movin' behind this assay office—us and the hosses. We'll be stayin' there, nice and quiet, till the company leaves. Start movin'!"

He gestured with his gun. Steve got out of the saddle and led both horses round the side of the assay office. Catsfoot followed him, Brogan on his heels. But all the time, Brogan's gun was trained on Steve.

They stood close against the rear wall. There they were completely concealed from anyone riding along the main street. Even if anyone actually entered the assay office they would not be seen unless he put his head out of the small back window —which would be unlikely.

Now Brogan was speaking in a whisper. He was saying: "If either of you makes any sound, it'll be the finish for both of you!"

Catsfoot's words were pitched low, but they were taunting as he asked: "You scared, Brogan? Mebbe if you'd been quick you could have got out of here before these folks arrived!"

Brogan bunched a fist and pulled it back. For a moment it looked as if he was about to hit Catsfoot. But he recovered his self-control.

"Yep, and mebbe I'd have been seen by them. This is the best way for me, Catsfoot, because whoever these hombres are, there's nothin' to keep 'em here. I figure they'll look around a bit after they've seen the dead men. But they won't find nothin'—not if you two are wise!"

Now the riders were in the street. The clink of bridle chains could be heard faintly but plainly. The hoofs were no longer beating steadily. They were making hesitant, squelching sounds as the animals were guided slowly and cautiously. Gradually, even that sound ceased. Steve guessed what was happening. They must be grouped round the bodies of the other brother and Gallota. But one tantalising question remained—who were those riders?

At that moment the question was answered. It came when the voice of one of the riders drifted towards them. A voice with the firm ring of the south-western territories.

"Seems our work's been done for us, sheriff. This sure is Gallota here and it looks like the other hombre had some kind of difference of opinion with him. Anyway, they killed each other."

Another voice said: "It's been a tough job findin' that knife pitcher, but I never figured on it endin' up this way. I don't suppose there's anyone else in this town, but we might as well take a quick look around then start back for Tucson. There's nothin' to keep us here and, anyway, the place makes me feel kind of creepy."

It was the posse which had been trailing Gallota!

Brogan's forefinger took more pressure on his gun trigger. He rammed the barrel into Steve's ribs.

He hissed: "Don't forget—one squeak out of either of you, and I shoot. . . !"

CHAPTER NINE

SHERIFF'S POSSE

THE sheriff's voice again drifted to them. They heard him say: "Sloan and Al—you two look in those stables. I figure you'll find their horses in there. The rest of us'll go on ahead."

"Okay, sheriff. We'll catch up with you in a couple of minutes."

Again hoofs squelched in the mud. Again bridle chains clinked. But now the sounds were much clearer and getting closer. The posse, naturally feeling confident that no one else was in the town, was making just a brief inspection by riding up the street. When they reached the other end of it, they would turn and ride out, never suspecting that three men were pressed against the wall at the back of the assay office. Never suspecting that two of them were being forced into silence by the threat of a killer's gun.

Unless . . .

Unless some noise could be made which would attract their attention. But any such noise would certainly mean that Brogan would squeeze the trigger. He did not make idle threats.

Now the posse was almost level with the front of the assay office—scarcely more than a dozen yards

away. Steve tried to summon the courage to call
out, even though it would be the last sound he
would ever make. Brogan must have sensed what
was going through his mind, for he clapped his free
hand over Steve's mouth. Steve felt his head
wrenched back until it was pressed against Brogan's
great chest. The grip was so fierce that he could
scarcely move a muscle.

It was Catsfoot who took a chance. He took a
chance with Steve's life as well as his own.
Cautiously, he drew back a foot. Then he made a
short, backward kick towards the horse which was
standing next to him. The spurred heel caught
against the animal's rear fetlock. It was far from
being a hard kick and it did not do the horse any
harm. But it was just enough to cause it a momen-
tary spasm of pain. Sufficient, he hoped, to make it
whinny. A horse may whinny at almost any time.
So perhaps this would look like pure chance.

That was how it happened. The animal showed
the whites of its eyes, splayed its nostrils. Then it
gave a brief, quivering snort.

Brogan made a fast half-turn, carrying Steve with
him. He glared at the animal and whispered something under his breath. Then, pressing the gun
even harder between Steve's ribs, he waited.
Waited to know whether the sound had been heard.

It had not been heard. That became obvious
within a few moments. The posse men were con-
tinuing to ride on and already they were past the
front of the office. That faint whinny had been

drowned by the talk among the riders themselves, as they discussed the fate of Gallota.

Catsfoot had to suppress a sigh of desperation. And the humourless smile spread on Brogan's lips. But it did not stay there for long. More horses were approaching, this time ridden at a gentle canter. All of them realised that these must be the men who had been ordered to look at the stables. Catsfoot thought of trying the same move again, but he immediately dismissed the idea. Brogan had not suspected the first time. A second attempt would be tempting fate too far.

But these two riders had suddenly halted. Judging by the sound, they had reined in directly in front of the office.

One of them said: "Looks like it's just been left around."

And the other answered: "It ain't been left here so long. . . ."

There was a creak of strained stirrup leathers. They were dismounting. Then another and a different type of creak as they stood on the decaying boardwalk. After that, a brief silence. The two must be looking at something. Steve managed to turn his head a fraction to glance at Catsfoot. Yes, Catsfoot knew what it was they had found. There was something about his taut expression which told Steve that.

Then they all knew.

One of the men shouted from the boardwalk. He shouted towards the rest of the posse, which by this time must have reached the distant end of the street.

"Hey, come back here!"

From far off the sheriff called: "What is it, Sloan?"

"We've picked up a gun from this boardwalk. It's one of the new Peacemakers . . . and sheriff, by the smell of it, I'd say it was used not so long ago!"

Steve felt an almost unbearable mixture of relief and fear. Catsfoot's gun—the gun Brogan had ordered him to drop—had been seen! He could hear the main body of the posse galloping back to the assay office. Now, for a certainty, they would make a thorough search of every building.

For the merest moment Brogan hesitated, his gun still thrust into Steve's body. Then he whipped his hand away from Steve's mouth and gave him a vicious push. It was a push which was intended to send him staggering against Catsfoot, so that both would sprawl helplessly on the ground. But Catsfoot had moved. He had swayed just a few vital inches, so that Steve floundered past him.

Brogan was already in the saddle of the nearest horse. He was still holding his gun, but not attempting to use it. If he did so, he would immediately pin-point his position to the posse. But he wanted the best chance of a clear getaway—and that meant silencing Catsfoot and Steve.

He tried to use his horse to do it.

Brogan jerked round the animal's head. At the same time, he pressed in his spurs. The horse rushed directly at Catsfoot and Steve. Catsfoot was the nearest, although less than a couple of feet separated the two. It seemed certain that both would be knocked down by the big animal and suffer injuries under its hoofs—perhaps even be killed by them.

Three factors saved them. They were Catsfoot's quicksilver mind, his speed on his feet, and his lacerated right hand. There was only the smallest fraction of a second in which to think and act. In that time, Catsfoot did both. He did not attempt to retreat from the horse. Instead, he flung himself at it, arm outstretched to grasp the bridle leather. Instinctively, the animal reared. At the same time, Catsfoot's fingers contacted the left rein at the point where it joined the bit chain. He wrenched it sideways. The horse, already almost upright, spun on its haunches, dragging the leather from Catsfoot's hand. But the double movement had been too much even for such an experienced horseman as Brogan. He tried to remain seated by grabbing the saddle pommel, flinging out his gun hand to keep balance. That hand crashed against the wall of the assay office. He gave a grunt of pain which was drowned by an explosion as a convulsive tightening of his finger pulled the trigger. The slug soared high and harmlessly through the air.

And Brogan was falling. Falling face first on to the muddy earth. He landed there like a great stone and lay still, all breath knocked out of him.

Steve rushed forward, got hold of the horse's head and calmed it. Catsfoot was standing over Brogan when the first of the posse thundered round the side of the building. They reined in, forming a tight circle round the group.

The sheriff looked at Brogan, who was now crawling unsteadily to his feet. Then at Catsfoot and Steve.

"I figure there's a lot of explainin' to do," he said to Catsfoot."

"I figure there is," Catsfoot said, "and I'll begin right now. . . ."

Two days later, Catsfoot and Steve sighted the tall wooden stockades of Fort Coulter. They saw the sentries on the ramparts and Old Glory flapping gently on the tall flagpole.

When they were still several hundred yards away, the great double gates swung open. An officer and six troopers galloped towards them.

"That's the captain of the guard!" Steve said urgently.

"I know it," Catsfoot answered, smiling. "But it doesn't worry me any—I'm not in the army."

Steve was not listening. He was buttoning the collar of his tattered tunic and setting his cap straight. He saluted crisply as the captain reined in.

"Bugler Steve Reynold, sir, from Lieutenant Anderson's column, reporting back."

The captain returned the salute. "Glad to see you safe, Reynold. Seems like you've had quite a time."

"Yep, it's been . . . quite a time, sir."

"And it's good to meet you again, Catsfoot," the captain added. Then he gazed at the big, unshaven man who was slumped on his horse between them. "But who's this you've brought along? He seems kind of familiar to me."

"That's one of the Brogan brothers," Catsfoot said. "Another of them's wounded also, and there's a chance of seeing him. The third's dead."

The captain slapped his thigh. "Say, this sure is something! We've been wanting to lay hands on the Brogans for a long time and . . ."

Catsfoot interrupted. "I want to know about something a whole lot more important, captain. I'm talking about a bunch of pioneers from a wagon train. Have any of them reached the fort in the last two or three days?

The captain gave Catsfoot a slow smile. Then he turned in his saddle and pointed back to the fort. "There's your answer," he said.

A crowd of people were streaming out of the gates and running towards them—most of them men, but women and children were there, too. It seemed that all of them were calling Catsfoot's name.

"They all got here safely," the captain said.

"And Lieutenant Anderson?"

"He'll be returned to duty in due time. He's doing fine. Right now, he's in the fort sick bay— where you'll be going to have those wounds of yours put right."

They could not talk any more, for the pioneers were swarming round Catsfoot, Luke well to the front. In a tumult of voices, they were thanking him, putting eager questions to him, telling him about their escape. Then, when they saw his wounds, a silence fell over them. But not for long, soon they were again chattering excitedly as they helped escort Catsfoot, Steve and the prisoner into the fort.

For Steve, the best moment of all came when they entered the fort compound. It was then that a great crash of musketry cut the hot air. It came from a hurriedly assembled guard of honour. They were firing a salute to the trail scout and the bugle boy.

That night, it seemed as if all would be quiet at Fort Coulter.

The pioneers, who were awaiting a new wagon train, were sleeping in emergency bunks which had been put up for them in the quartermaster's building. Because the medical officer said that he needed rest, Steve was in the sick bay with Catsfoot and Lieutenant Anderson. On the lonely ramparts, sentries trudged, hunching their shoulders against the cold wind.

It was the sentry on the east wall who gave the alarm.

First he heard the thudding of approaching ponies. Straining his eyes through the darkness, he saw the silhouettes of four riders. They were making straight for the fort. But, so far as he could see, there was no more than four of them. . . .

Puzzled, the sentry unslung his Spencer carbine.

Raising the barrel high in the air, he discharged a single shot—the emergency warning.

Fort Coulter sprang to urgent life.

Troopers streamed out of the guardroom, which was just within the main gates. Buckling on their ammunition belts, they rushed up the wooden steps to the ramparts. Within a minute, a dozen grim-faced men were kneeling on each of the walls, rifles sighted. And from the main barrack building, the rest of the garrison were emerging to take up their action posts.

On the east wall, a corporal was in temporary command.

"Hold your fire!" he shouted.

A nearby trooper gave a glare of disgust.

"Hold fire! Why? They look like Injuns to me!"

"Four of 'em ain't goin' to hurt us—and it seems like one of 'em's got a white flag."

The corporal was right on both counts. The four riders reined in while fifty yards from the wall and in the thin moonlight a square of white material could be discerned fastened to the lance which one of them was holding. It was the man with the lance who called towards the fort.

"We come in peace," he said, "on the bidding of Earo. Let me alone enter that I may tell you Earo's words."

Now the commanding officer was on the east rampart. He was a hard man, this Colonel Sangster, with no reason to like the Apaches. But he was also a fair one.

He said half to himself: "I don't like having even one Apache in this fort, but I guess I'll have to let him in." Then, raising his voice, he called an order: "Open the gates—then shut them again just as soon as he's inside."

Four troopers raised the huge beam which secured the gates. Spencers ready at their waists, they fell into position at each side of the entrance as the Apache advanced. He did so slowly, his lance with the white cloth attached to it, still held aloft. He looked straight ahead, his copper-hued face expressionless, as he entered the fort compound and halted his pony. Behind him, the gates were dragged shut.

Colonel Sangster came down from the ramparts. One hand on his sabre, he strode towards the Indian. At the same moment, Catsfoot emerged from the sick bay, Steve at his side. Catsfoot's buckskin jacket was thrown loosely over his bare shoulders, showing his freshly bandaged left arm suspended from a sling. New bandages were also over his right hand. He and Steve joined the colonel, all three standing directly in front of the Apache.

"Get on with it," the colonel snapped. "What's this message?"

The Apache inclined his head slightly towards Catsfoot. "It was to you that Earo made a pledge," he said tonelessly.

"He did just that," Catsfoot agreed. "He promised to return the last of the Brogan brothers. Have you brought him with you?"

"It is so. He waits outside with two of our warriors."

"Then why haven't you handed him over right away?"

"Because Earo commands me to remind you that his pledge was to deliver this man to you. This he does with a glad heart, for he is of no more use to our people. But know this—when he was told he was to be taken to you, he tried to flee."

The colonel grunted: "That doesn't surprise me any," he said.

"He tried to seize a pony and while doing so he slew one of our braves. For that he must face our justice. He must die at our hands!"

There was a long silence. Then Catsfoot asked quietly: "Is he still alive?"

"Yes, he lives. But before many minutes have passed we will slay him. It is good that it should be so."

"Let's get this straight—you mean you intend finishing him right outside this fort?"

"It is so. It is Earo's wish that you see with your own eyes that we, too, do justice."

Catsfoot breathed heavily. "But Earo will be breaking his word if this is done! He promised to deliver this man to us!"

"Earo always keeps his pledge. The white man will be left outside these walls. But he will be dead."

Catsfoot and the colonel looked at each other. Each knew that they could not stand by and let Apache knives kill this man within sight of the fort.

Neither of them doubted that the Brogan had indeed slain an Apache, just as he had used his guns against many whites before that. But he was entitled to a fair trial—in the same way as his brother, who was at this moment in the fort jail.

The colonel said: "He must be handed over to us alive! In due time he'll go to Tucson and face a judge and jury. There's a load of evidence against him and the other brother, so you don't need to worry none about justice. Those two will hang just as sure as to-morrow will come."

The Apache stared ahead, unmoved. "One of them may hang," he said. "The other will perish by the knife . . ." He drew a blade from beneath his sash and it glittered in the moonlight. "I return now to do Earo's bidding. Open the gates."

He turned his pony, but Colonel Sangster gripped the bridle, bringing the animal to a stop.

"Get this," he said. "You're not leaving here until I have your word that the prisoner will not be harmed by you!"

The Apache stared at the tip of his lance. "You talk of justice—yet you would seize me when I come to you in peace?"

His words were laden with contempt. And immediately a new factor became obvious to the colonel and Catsfoot—they could not try to save the prisoner by holding this Apache. If they did so, the Apaches would never again have confidence in the word of the army. And it would be unlikely to save the brother, in any case.

The colonel made a last effort. "Very well, you can go. But if you carry out this threat it will be remembered and you will pay."

The Apache shrugged and kneed his pony towards the gates, which were reopening.

Steve had listened silently. Now he said urgently to Catsfoot: "This . . . this'll be awful!"

"I know it, son."

"That Brogan deserves to die, just like the others. But he must . . . must . . ." He broke off, groping for words.

"You mean, he must have the right to speak for himself," Catsfoot put in. "The right of a trial. That's the rule of law—and I guess it's what we're fighting to establish in this territory. If we let the Apaches do this, right outside an army fort, a lot of folks are going to lose faith in us."

"But what can we do?"

Catsfoot turned to the colonel. He said: "I'd like to borrow your gun, sir, seeing I haven't mine with me."

Colonel Sangster's tough face crinkled in surprise.

"What d'you want it for? Anyway, you can't use it. Not with a pair of hurt hands."

"My right hand's not so bad, colonel. I can't use it to draw fast. But it's improved a lot in the last couple of days and I figure I can aim straighter than any man in the territory. So just loan me your gun, colonel."

"Don't talk crazy, Catsfoot! You can't start shooting up those Apaches! It's like that Injun said

—they're protected because they're under a white flag."

"I won't shoot anyone. Just trust me. I have an idea and I think mebbe it'll give that hombre just a chance of reaching us alive and having a fair trial."

The colonel hesitated. Then he pulled his ·45 from a black leather holster and handed it to Catsfoot. "I sure hope you know what you're doing," he said.

But Catsfoot did not answer. Already he was moving through the open gates. Moving with those long, silent strides. Following the Apache who had just ridden out.

Steve called out and tried to follow him. But the colonel gripped his shoulder, holding him back.

"I don't know what's in Catsfoot's mind," he said. "But you won't help him any by making a noise and trailing him around. This is where we can do nothing but wait."

Steve looked in anguish at the colonel. "But he's risking his life just so that killer will get a fair deal! I didn't think he'd try anything like this—not try to handle it alone! It's crazy!"

The colonel gave an order for the gates to be kept open. Then he turned again to Steve.

"I guess you're right, son. But that's Catsfoot. I figure it's just one of the things that make him different from ordinary folk. . . ."

Fear—cold, damp and paralysing—gripped every

nerve in that Brogan's body. He was partly slumped over the neck of his pony. Sometimes his eyes rolled to either side, to look at the braves who guarded him. Or they stared straight ahead at the third Apache, who was slowly returning from the fort. He knew what was to happen, for they had told him. When that brave reached them a knife would be used. He would die within sight of the fort—with soldiers looking on. And no one able to help him.

"But they *should* be able to help!" he told himself amid the fevered chaos of his mind. "They can't let this happen to me! Not like this. . . ."

It was typical of him that he now expected help from those he had betrayed.

The third Apache had almost reached them. He had halted his pony only a few yards in front of them, his back to the fort. He flicked his left wrist and the lance with its piece of white cloth dug deep into the earth. Then the Brogan looked at the other hand. It held a knife—a curved and glinting knife.

The Brogan brother tried to utter words of pleading. None would come. He could only moan.

The Apache looked at him with contempt. He did not see—none of them saw—the ghost-like figure, bent almost double, which was approaching directly behind him. He edged his pony closer to the Brogan brother, to be within easy striking distance. He drew back the blade, preparing for the final thrust. . . .

The knife disintegrated. It shattered into scores of jagged fragments. At the same time, the crash of a ·45 swept over the sage.

Catsfoot was standing a dozen paces away. Standing with his buckskin jacket still draped loosely over his shoulders. To the Brogan brother and to the Apaches, it seemed that he had materialised out of the solid earth.

The explosion had not faded when Catsfoot shouted.

"Ride for the fort, Brogan! Ride . . . !"

At first, the man did nothing. Like the three others, he blinked stupidly at Catsfoot. Then all of them recovered their wits at the same time. The Brogan kneed his pony forward in the uncertain start of a gallop. And the three Apaches closed in on him. One of them was holding a horn-handle tomahawk. It's slender, razor-edged head was streaking towards the Brogan's neck. Then the tomahawk, too, vanished. A ·45 slug wrenched it out of the Apache's hand.

Somehow, amid renewed confusion, Brogan forced his pony clear of the Apaches. He galloped for the open gates of the fort, stretched almost flat along the animal's mane. But the Apaches had forgotten him. Their fury was turned upon Catsfoot.

And Catsfoot was retreating, too.

He was walking slowly backwards, his gun levelled at the Indians. The Indians were pulling rifles from their saddle clasps. A few more seconds and they would be using them—aiming a fusillade at him. Catsfoot realised that his only chance was to shoot first—and shoot to kill. But he could not do that. He might blow the rifles out of their hands, just as he had destroyed the knife and the tomahawk. But in the end the Apaches would get him long before he could reach the fort.

It was then that he heard a familiar, reassuring sound. It came from the gates—the thud of galloping hoofs. Not the unshod hoofs of Indian ponies, but of big cavalry mounts. It was a temptation to look round, but Catsfoot resisted it. He kept the ·45 trained on the Apaches. He saw their hands freeze on their rifles, their bodies become rigid. Then, suddenly, he could see them no more. . . .

A column of twenty troopers were turning in front of him. They reined in when they had formed a solid line between Catsfoot and the Apaches.

The captain of the guard had drawn his sabre. He pointed it at the three Indians and told them: "You came here under a flag of truce to deliver a white prisoner. The prisoner's in the fort and so far no one's been hurt. Let's keep it that way!"

The spokesman for the Apaches looked at his rifle. Then, very deliberately, he pushed it back into the leather clasp. His tones were heavy with hatred as he said: "You have thwarted our justice! You have let a white man who has slain one of our people go free!"

"He's not free. Right now, he'll be joining his

brother in the fort jail and there he'll stay until he's moved to Tucson for a trial."

But the Apache was not impressed. Probably he did not understand. He said: "This will not be forgotten by my people . . ."

Then the three turned their ponies and rode away into the night. Rode with a message for Earo.

In the commanding officer's office, Catsfoot handed over the ·45. "Thanks for the loan, colonel. And thanks for sending out the troopers. That was fast work. If you hadn't done it, I'd never have got back here."

The colonel lit a cheroot and sat on a corner of his desk. "I'm wondering if we haven't all been a bit crazy. We've given the Apaches another grudge against us, and what for? Just to save that outlaw from the Apaches."

"There was a lot more in it than that—and you know it," Catsfoot said. "There was that little something that we call justice. It's got to apply to everyone, even folks like the Brogans. I figure it's worth most any risk."

The colonel puffed out a dense cloud of smoke and smiled. "You're right—but I hope the justice the Brogans will get will be mighty tough."

"I figure it will be, sir. But that's not our worry. We can leave that to a judge and jury in Tucson. Now I'm going to get myself some sleep. I'm tired."

He strode out of the colonel's office and back to the sick bay, where Steve was waiting for him.